I0721333

Dita

by
Greg Randall

AOS Publishing, 2023

Copyright © 2023

Greg Randall

All rights reserved under International
and Pan-American copyright conventions

ISBN: 978-1-990496-19-6

Cover Design: Chanelle Poupart

Visit AOS Publishing's website:
www.aospublishing.com

Dedication

I dedicate this book to Jeff Scott, who has provided me with vintage motorcycles that have demanded more of me mechanically than I could ever offer back to them.

— You'll learn, he said. I have faith in you.

What I know about twisting wrenches is because of his patient refusal to let me sit idling by while he did the work.

I suspect he and my ICU nurse wife, Sandy, had a secret agreement. He would supply me with bikes that I could shine and polish in the cool of my garage but would falter and die as soon as I attempted to take them out on the road.

Jeff has pushed bikes further than I have ridden them, and for that, Sandy thanks him. He kept his part of the bargain.

I continue to hope for an open road, sweeping curves, and vistas that reach beyond the horizon. I dream about a thoroughly modern 650 *Africa Twin* or a *KTM Dual Sport*. Because the jury's out on which one I prefer, I'll take both! A second motorcycle would do nicely. And a doghouse to sleep in.

Part One

1

Blauer Würger
(Blue Strangler)

Dita pulled out her pack of *Juwell 72s*. She lit one and offered it to Inge.

Mesmerized by the bright red lipstick on the filter, Inge wondered if she would burst into flame from the smell of oil and *Benzin* (gasoline) that hung in the air.

She shook her head.

— Those things will kill you, Dita.

She took a long drag and blew smoke rings out her tail pipe.

— Bet you can't do that, eh? On the track or off, expansion chambers are my secret weapon. When they sing, I fly.

While Inge shifted from foot to foot, Dita rested on her centre stand.

They stood under the shade of an old oak tree at the far side of the motorcycle factory parking lot in Zschopau, Saxony, East Germany where Dita first received the spark of light that brought her to life. They watched Inge's son Norbert setting stones loose from his sling shot. He hit a glass bottle on a fence post near the trees. It exploded into hundreds of reflecting green shards that glittered in the sunlight.

— Good eye, Norbi! Dita yelled. It's all in that new rubber tubing, isn't it?

Inge beamed.

The boy cast a shy glance back. He grabbed a handful of stones and went off in search of a giant. He wanted *des Jägers Ehrenschild* (the Hunter's Honour). It was time for him to become a man, and he had to do something big. He needed to draw blood that wasn't his own.

— Sling shots are safer than motorcycles, Dita reflected. The longer you keep your boy off them, the better. We two-wheelers require loving and fearing. Something he has yet to learn.

— And not the hard way, I hope, Inge said. Childhood is a precious fleeting time. A few short years at best. I'd like to create a trove of memories that he will treasure. Maybe even replace the horde he amassed from the war.

— It's a losing battle, you know. Hoping your son will follow the path you choose for him. One day, you'll have to let him go, not today of course, but it will come sooner than you think.

— That's the parent's privilege, setting their children free. Is it too much to ask, though? To raise a son who is *ein freundlicher Mann* (one who treats women gently)?

— You're kidding, right? When he's surrounded by motorcycling matadors? Men who are fully alive only when they are on the track or riding pillion with their lover?

— That's the rub, isn't it? My son growing up with racers who face death in leathers—like bullfighters in their *traje de luces* (suit of lights).

— One thing that's appealing about Spaniards in the face of great danger. They carry themselves with grace and majesty. Matadors compete on the sand floor of an arena. They face a bull within two concentric circles of chalk, a little world made cunningly. It is a microcosm of violence, self-contained yet universal. Motorcycling and bullfighting aren't just games. They occur in red zones that lead to death. There is a dignity in accepting the inevitable.

Thwack! A stone hit a branch and fell through the leaves to the ground, scaring off a fox.

— Why is the shedding of blood such a necessary human rite? Inge wondered. Girls bleed and become women. Boys draw blood and become men. They beget great joy, pain, and suffering. The weal and the woe of the world are both covered in red.

— Neither a sport nor an entertainment but something real. Bloodletting gives hope for immortality in our temporal bodies.

— All the folk tales I've heard demand sacrifice. Someone must die, or an injustice must be committed.

— Listeners expect no less than a wounding of the soul. Otherwise, the stories they hear are tales told by idiots, full of sound and signifying nothing.

— What is true in myth is also true in sport. Bullfighting and motorcycle racing thrill and horrify yet hypnotize with sacramental display.

— We can't look away. We are mesmerized.

— Ritual speaks out our distress. A liturgy with or without faith, it shouts from rooftops our inmost fears. Speaking our pain out loud brings solace. We are relieved. Life could be so much worse, but it isn't, and that is all that matters.

— People in pain plead forgiveness for the guilt they feel. Their heart's cry is a prayerful outpouring, not unlike the *Cante* (Deep Song) in Flamenco.

Inge grabbed the smoke from Dita and took a quick puff.

— When people witness the death of a hero, they sing out their anguish to an indifferent God.

She handed the cigarette back.

— I could get addicted to these.

— True power in sport is in its ability to excite the audience. Poor plays and bad calls incite fans to outrage. It's involuntary. They have no choice but to react.

— Like the red of the *muleta*?

— Fuchsia, yellow, green, blue, or purple, the tint or hue of the cape doesn't matter. The bull cannot distinguish colour. The matador begins the fight with the short *capote de brega*. When he switches to the longer red cape, the audience knows that the Third Act is about to begin.

— The soul-wrenching wail of the *Duende* (the mystical power of the singer to draw in the audience) and the skirl of the two-stroke motorcycle engine are one and the same. The matador is still as steel, and the motorcyclist is unflinching. They negotiate a thin red line between life and death. The fans may not speak it, they may not admit it; but they want it! They pray for the falling of the other. The spectacle of someone else's suffering electrifies them. An innocent man crucified, a body prone in flames, a matador gored badly, or a bull killed poorly. These are the icons of an ultimate sacrifice, a life given for the sake of others.

— We breathe a sigh of relief that it is not us.

— All the world's a stage and all the men and women merely players. There is no escaping the final exit.

— *Blut fordert Blut haben* (Blood will have blood), Dita said.

A stone whizzed over their heads. They ducked.

Inge looked up and saw her son.

— Not toward us, Norbert! She yelled with panic in her voice. Out into the field! No! Not this way!

— Sorry, Mama!

— Do I need to confiscate your weapon? I don't want you denting Dita's tank.

— Oh, don't you worry about me, *Tante* Inge (Aunty Inge). That'd be just the thing to have Hackebeil work his magic on my top. He can slip his hands under my fairing any day of the week.

— Shut up, Dita! Inge laughed. You're not talking about Hackebeil? The sheet metal worker!

— Dieter, my love.

— You're a strange piece of handiwork, Inge said, mocking her friend.

Dita gave her the eye.

Norbert turned away from Dita and his mother and fired off another stone.

Clang. It hit a traffic sign.

Inge grimaced, watching her son stalk the villainous Rattler in the Karl May novels he'd been reading. She shuddered at the memory of the blood-crazed drunken soldier who burst through her door during the last days of the war.

She's hated the Russians ever since.

Dita's voice pulled Inge out of her nightmare.

— *Tante, was ist los* (what's the matter)?

She turned toward her son, tears running down her face.

— Kill the bastard, Norbi.

Inge seized the cigarette and took a long drag. Then she coughed.

— Such terrible that happened to Karl Lottes. He was invincible on the track, whether riding a *DKW*, Mondial, or *MV Agusta*.

— The highest-rated German privateer on the Continental Circuit. Then to end his career on the *Nordschleife* (the north loop on the Nürburgring). It's unthinkable.

— As much as I loathed competing against him, I loved what he could do with two wheels. How I wish I had him in my saddle.

— A Sam Hawkens to teach you what you don't know how?

— I prefer Italians to Germans. Real men like Carlo Ubbiali and Tarquino Provini.

— But have you ever met one? Inge asked. Give me a Jürgen, Klaus, or Günter any day over one of those. Yours sound like phantasms from an overheated imagination.

— Shut your mouth, *Meine Lieblingstante* (My favourite aunt), Dita interrupted. Don't ruin everything. I'm still dreaming about Alfredo, Carlo, Giuseppe, and oh-my-God Umberto.

— Norbert Kaaden, no! Inge yelled. Not towards the parking lot!

Norbert crawled away on his hands and knees, picking off Cavalry snipers. Those bastards deserve scalping. The way they treat their women.

— Maybe I shouldn't let him read all those novels about Winnetou and Old Shatterhand.

Inge heard a whizzing sound fly over her head. She ducked behind Dita. The exploding of a stone hitting an automobile windshield startled her.

— Oh shit, Dita, Inge whispered. Norbert just took out Hartmann's car.

— What the...?

Dita's engine fired without hesitation. Inge grabbed the handlebars, pushed Dita off the centre stand, and jumped on.

— Grab Norbi as I swing by.

— They giggled like nervous schoolgirls, running away from their teacher's disapproving glare.

Norbert's eyes opened wide as his Mum dragged him by his sweater up on the bike behind her.

— Hang on tight, she yelled. Her skirt hitched up past her knees with her legs astride Dita's voluptuous hand-hammered aluminum fuel tank.

She twisted the throttle and Dita belched out a stream of blue invective. Her street ready *Continentals* spun in the gravel as they sped out of the parking lot. Dust billowed behind them.

Inge laughed, and Norbert cried as he tucked the slingshot deep into his jacket pocket. He didn't know what to make of his mother, or Dita for that matter. He'd never before seen them so wound-up.

Dita didn't stop vibrating until Inge pushed her into the old shed, turned the engine off and closed the fuel petcock.

Inge pulled her terrified son into the house.

He needed a bath, Dita needed to cool down, and she needed a very tall glass of *Blauer Würger* to settle her nerves.

Surely there was a bottle with the blue coloured label tucked somewhere in the kitchen cupboard for a moment just like this. She let out a sigh when she saw the vodka hidden behind a jar of poppy seeds.

— I will stand, no matter what comes my way, Inge vowed. Eventually. But right now, I need a drink more than I need anything in this world.

2

Jungs bleiben Jungs
(Boys Will Be Boys)

The next morning, Dita eased herself into the kitchen and rolled over to the table. Inge, nursing a headache, set a cup of strong black coffee in front of the trim, well-built motorcycle, and her rather magnificent handlebars.

Dita pushed it away.

— I prefer something with less octane.

Inge ignored her.

— Hurry, son, you don't want to be late.

— How are you doing, Norbi? Dita asked.

— Papa phoned Herr Hartmann as soon as he got home.

— What did he say?

— He laughed.

Dita looked at Inge.

She shrugged.

— Boys will be boys, he said. And Mums who give their sons slingshots should be given citizenship awards. He even promised me a ride in his new car! He didn't care about the old windshield. There was already a crack in in. I promised from now on to practice at the shooting range. He wants me to try out for the Olympic team.

— Time for school, young man.

Norbert gave Dita a quick peck, grabbed his satchel, and ran for the door.

— Hey, Inge said. Aren't you forgetting something?

— *Tut mir leid, Mama* (I'm sorry). He turned back to his mother and gave her the kind of hug only a child can give an adult. One filled with absolution, healing, and unconditional love. Inge's heart melted within her. She did not want to let him go, it felt so good. This hug of redemption.

— *Bitte* (Please), I've got to hurry. My friends are waiting. He wriggled away from her and burst out of the house, slamming the door behind him.

— I can finally relax, Inge sighed, as she sat at the table and nursed her coffee.

— Did Hartmann really have a change of heart?

— Not really. He just knows that Walter is his ticket out of here.

— You don't really think he's considering...

— Defecting? No, not that. He's a man who hungers and thirsts for power. If he fled to the West, he'd disappear into obscurity. Here he's *Der große Mann* (the big man).

The door opened, and Walter stepped in.

— Good morning, ladies. Finally up? It's brisk out there.

— *Morgen, Onkel* Walter.

He kissed Inge on the cheek and sat beside Dita. How are you doing, old girl?

Silently, she passed him some gas.

— Good Lord, Walter said. I think you need to go for a good run.

— Don't you bother! Spending all this time with *Tante* Inge, I have a sudden hankering for someone who will love me for what I am, not for how fast I can go. I need a lover who will stay with me after a podium finish.

— You've done your Sunday racing. Now, it's your Monday scheming?

— Every minute of the day.

— You seem in fine spirits after what happened.

— Hartmann wasn't upset?

— He laughed. Said Norbert reminded him of when he was a child.

— The tomfoolery a boy can get into when he has a slingshot!

— Exactly. It's only a windshield, Hartmann assured me. Nothing to fuss about. He's more concerned that we win a *World Championship.*

— So, we're in the clear? Inge asked. Can we get on with our lives?

— Without a doubt.

— All I know is that if we're going to survive the Continental Circuit, we have to keep our wits about us, Dita said. We can't be too careful.

— And how do we do that?

— Accept that we're pawns in this game. Things won't go exactly as planned. Politicians will use us for political ends. We need to play according to their expectations, not ours.

Walter stubbed out his cigarette.

— If we don't bring home a *World Championship,* there is no hope.

— Our young team can adapt. They aren't saddled with old fears and missed opportunities. Brehme, Fügner, and Musiol assume they can win every race they enter. They just need machines that run perfectly every time.

— Well, you can have Musiol as far as I am concerned, Dita said.

— Huh! Why's that? Walter asked.

— Men in uniforms have never been kind to me.

— Me neither, said Inge. I hate soldiers. They rape women and butcher innocent children.

— Musiol is a proud member of the *VoPo* (*Volkspolizei*, the East German national police force) and a top motorcycle racer, Walter said. He's as good as they get. The people love him, so does Berlin.

— I can't stand what he represents, Dita said.

— And what exactly is that?

— An ever-deepening line through No-Man's Land. Barriers built to impede progress. People who build fences have a nostalgic understanding of the past and an uncompromising hope for the future.

— All I know, Inge said, is that we're about to blast off and a cold war between the East and the West is heating up.

— Time is of the essence. We need to work quickly. There's no telling when this will all come to an end.

— Oh, for the days when we could tour Europe's capitals and not be afraid, Walter said. Instead, Americans cower inside bomb shelters. Europeans stock pantry shelves. East Germans are under orders to become gold medal winners in every sport they enter.

— We start with Saarland and make a showing at Monza, Dita said. Then we try our best at the Isle of Man.

— Win, show, or place, the odds are against us.

— They've never been in our favour.

— Sometimes just getting out of bed is good enough.

— Then we must do our own work in our own way because we are responsible for both.

3

Durch eine Schikane
(Through One Chicane)

It was clear to the West German businessman and motorcycle engine tuner Paul Petry that the old Communist Bernhard Petruschke was having trouble on the track with the new full fairing on his *MZ* (*Motorrad Zschopau*) motorcycle.

Petry used his relationship with the organizer of the Saarland race to meet Walter Kaaden. He had hoped to sell fiery *MZs* in the West. They were inexpensive to buy and explosive to race. They just needed to be in the hands of an experienced rider.

Petruschke's younger teammate Horst Fügner seemed better able to cope with the gusting winds. Earlier that year on a cordoned-off section of the Autobahn outside Karl-Marx-Stadt, Fügner had blown off course when testing the new fairings from the Peisteritz Plastics plant. In this race, Fügner knew what to expect; Petrus did not.

Dita wedged herself between Walter and the handsome westerner.

— You need a wind tunnel, Petry said. Then you could deal with the aerodynamic challenges before the season starts, not during.

— The problem is not just with gusting winds but peering through distorted windscreens, Walter said. Our factory can't get the optics right.

— We need to see where we're going if we want to win, Dita said.

— However, we cannot allow these imperfections to keep us from racing. We've always fined tuned on the fly. That's why we bring the whole team along. To make the changes that circumstances demand. It's the only way.

— I can't imagine racing as a privateer without factory and team support. The rider is responsible for everything.

— The best riders know their machines and can use their tools. You can't do one without the other.

Walter trained his racers to be self-sufficient and adaptable to the changing conditions of each competition. No two races were ever the same. The only way to get more funding from Berlin was to increase their podium finishes. They needed to know how much they could push their machines before redlining the engines. Instinct informed by knowledge and hands-on practical experience are essential to winning on the Continental Circuit.

— In the meantime, we make do.

— I know a plastics company in Bologna, Petry said. If you pay in cash, they'll sidestep the sanctions against East German. They have what you want.

— Then Berlin better make good on its promise to get us a big transport truck. We need to prepare for this year's race at Monza and next year's season starter in Spain.

— I can hardly wait for the Isle of Man, Dita said. Racing its thirty-seven miles has long been every motorcyclist's dream.

— 37 POINT 739 miles, Petry said, correcting her.

— I love the Triskelion on their flag, Dita continued, ignoring him. Its three legs running clockwise and their motto *Whichever Way You Throw, It Will Stand.*

The Manx could be East German, she thought, They're so resilient.

4

Der Schlüssel zum Sieg
(The Key to Victory)

Dita loved riding shotgun on the team bus. But she had to admit that getting up the front steps was tricky. Eventually, however, Brehme and Hackebeil heaved, pulled, and manhandled her into position.

— Hey, boys! Watch it! You're getting rude. She laughed with pleasure as they blushed red-hot, thrilled to touch the mystery of her unfaired chassis. Finding purchase with their hands, clutching her well-wrought frame, they jostled her into the window seat.

— Dita, it's a good thing you're such a fine slip of a thing, Brehme said. Getting you up these stairs has thrown my back out. If you were any heavier, I'd have to retire before we get to Monza.

— Is a 250 too much for you to handle? Maybe you need to stay with a 125.

— The smaller the bike, the more exciting the ride. I bet a 50cc'd go like stink. They may be small, but they are mighty.

— And as fierce as a wild cat, Dita said. Too bad those piddlers aren't quite ready for the track.

The boys eased Dita into place.

— Glad you took out the front seat for me. I couldn't have wiggled into the cramped quarters you two-leggers fold yourselves into. Two-wheelers need room for angling.

— And ogling?

— Bet you can't believe this is happening, Hackebeil said.

— What do you mean, *Schatzi* (darling)?

— That we're going to Italy.

— The sun, the roads, the gorgeous men?

— No! That we're racing our first *GP!*

— Oh that. It's always been a foregone conclusion. We can do no other. It's the one chance we have to fulfill our destiny. But first we must find the way.

— The way to the podium? The way to fame and glory?

— The way to winning! That's where my hope comes from. Not from some pie in the sky faith in the unknown. The sound of crisp banknotes in my billfold gives me the faith I need to continue.

— There isn't always a direct way to the top. Sometimes you have to lose yourself to find your way.

— A Loser's Circle? That's not exactly my cup of tea.

— What I want to know is why we couldn't drive through Switzerland? Maybe visit Taveri's hometown? He's quite the doll.

— And risk the Splüger Pass? You're completely off your rockers. It has a 13% grade at 2100 metres.

— I don't have rockers, you idiot. I'm divine simplicity. A two-stroke without valves, just ports and channels and Uncle Walter's magic.

— We'd be crazy to go that way. The Brenner's our only option at 1300 metres. Even then, this old bus might not make it.

— Maybe Taveri's already at Monza. Then we could go at it *mano a mano* (hand to hand) or even better, face to face.

— Until death do you part?

— He's a stellar motorcyclist. He can put his Swiss hand to my German throttle any minute of any day.

— Getting through border control is the tricky part. Once the Italians figure out who we are, they'll take their own sweet time. They won't let us pass until it is too late.

— Don't you worry boys. Let me exude some of my charm. Those Italians will be tickling my carburetor before you know it.

— No, Dita, no! her teammates all cried. We'd be lost in a quagmire. We wouldn't see the light of day until Monza is over. You stay here. We'll cover you with a tarp. They won't suspect a thing. They'll be looking through the big truck for our secret weapon, not at the front of the bus.

— Like those Greek soldiers wheeling their wooden horse up to the gates of Troy? The key to victory is what lurks inside, under the fairing.

5

Kostümprobe
(Dress Rehearsal)

The team anticipated delays at the border into Italy. But they hadn't counted on the numerous breakdowns the old bus would have during the trip south. The engine started knocking as the bus laboured up high mountain passes. The brakes overheated during the long descents. To lighten the load, the men transferred as much of the gear as they could to the truck. It helped but not much.

Dita, of course, stayed put while the capable men of the *Rennkollektiv* (Racing Team) repeatedly tore the broken-down bus apart and put it back together. They knew what they were doing, and Dita kept out of their way.

— I believe in the delegation of authority. As professionals, they'll do their jobs. I trust them.

When the bus reached the Italian border, Dita covered her top. Sadly, she drew no admiring glances from the men she could hitherto only have dreamt about. It seemed such a wasted opportunity to let these exquisite creatures slip by, but her sacrifice was, indeed, for the greater good.

She kept her yap shut.

The Italians watched with disdain as the East German caravan pulled up to the border. While one scrutinized the paperwork, another rifled through the truck. The last two climbed into the bus.

The shamble of men with greasy hands and rumpled clothes did not raise any suspicions. They were tired, unkempt, and relieved that the bus hadn't broken down while they were waiting in line.

One smartly dressed officer lifted Dita's tarp and gave her a dismissive glance.

Typical, he thought. These Sausage-Eaters have a ratty old parts bike up front, under an oil-stained shroud.

— She's our lucky charm, our relic they explained. We wouldn't dream of leaving her behind.

The Italians snorted. Standing on ceremony, they were arrogant and judgemental, and filled with contempt. Turning on their well-polished heels, they thundered down the stairs and off the bus, allowing the East Germans to cross the border.

Even though the *Rennkollektiv* arrived in Monza a day later than the other competitors, they managed to qualify in the last practice run

13

but just barely. They hadn't time to tune the bikes to the altitude, barometric pressure, or octane of the fuel that the officials supplied.

When the starter's pistol went off, the engines were running reasonably well, but nowhere near their peak performance. As a result, the team finished in the middle of the pack. Not one *MZ* came close to a podium finish. Their debut was mediocre at best and raised hardly a ripple in the stands. The press, however, had a heyday, making fun of the band of gypsies from East Germany.

Didn't their mechanics know how to set those carburetors? Those tail pipes are dreadful. Look at the shoddy fairings and cloudy windscreens. The men sleep in tents in the paddock and cook their meals on camp stoves. Those East Germans are an embarrassment and should not be allowed to participate in the *Grand Prix*. What were the organizers thinking?

All was not wasted, however. After their baptism at Monza, the *Rennkollektiv* made a side trip to Bologna where they met the supplier that Paul Petry said would do a cash deal.

Distortion-free windscreens would allow the riders to see clearly, so Walter doled out his crumpled supply of Deutschmarks one at a time.

— This is just a dress rehearsal, lads, he said. Ignore the headlines. We're here to get our feet wet. Introduce ourselves to the world. From the outset, we knew we couldn't compete against the likes of Carlo Ubbiali, Romolo Ferri, and Luigi Taveri.

That the transport truck had to tow the bus home from Sterzing in South Tyrol did not add insult to injury so much as it made their first run at a *World Championship* unforgettable. They had a long road ahead of them. The mockery at Monza had to happen. The West had to scoff at the *Rennkollektiv*.

Now, they could take part in the Continental Circus and the world would witness first-hand Walter's wizardry. Nothing could deter the *Rennkollektiv*. They were off and running.

6

Lebensmitte Nahtoderfahrung
(Mid-Life Death Experience)

Curse that wicked *Raidillon*! Followed by a downhill lefthander and an immediate uphill right. Damn the *Eau Rouge*! The most loved and feared corner at Spa-Francorchamps. The worst on the Continental Circuit.

It is always unforgiving and never allows any margin for error. Riders either face death at the front of the pack; or they are at the rear, losing the race of their lives.

The course followed a public road through town. Straw bales on curves were the only concession to safety. Motorcyclists skirted houses, flanked stone walls, and edged past steep embankments. Lightweight helmets and thin close-fitting leathers were no defence against concrete posts that stood stalwart while motorcycles rattled over rough, cobbled, and potholed streets.

Little thought was given to the rider's well-being and none whatsoever to the fans. Anyone could die. Death as always is no respecter of persons. It comes whether you pay the entry fee or not.

During the training runs, Dita gave the competition a run for its money. Western riders no longer took one look at her and dismissed her out of hand. They saw her for what she was: a force not to be taken lightly. They no longer ignored her but lusted mightily after her winsome ways.

Neither Petruschke nor Fügner went full throttle. They rode just fast enough to get through the qualifications. It is always better to have a bit more fire in the pan than the competition expects. As the race progressed, they drafted behind the leaders and forced them to go faster and faster until their engines faltered, and they fell out of the running.

The best way to win a race is to push the leaders so hard that they burnout their engines.

Walter's bikes may have been tricky to ride, but when they were operating perfectly, they were so robust that they could last longer than anything else on the track.

They won by enduring. *Ausdauer ist der Schlüssel* (Perseverance is the key).

Even though Dita was running as hot as she could, the weekend of 5 July 1959 turned out to be a nasty one. First, Petruschke hit an oil slick and caromed off the track. When he landed ass up on the grass unhurt, Dita breathed a sigh of relief.

— That old Communist must have nine lives.

Then Fügner moved into Petruschke's position and hooked onto Ubbiali's rear wheel. He followed him into the notorious *Linkskurve* (Left Curve) but misjudged the apex (the sharpest arc in a curve) and exited too quickly. Flying off his bike, he catapulted head over heels through the air. The handsome East German with the easy smile and open heart smashed headfirst into a light standard.

Dita stopped breathing as Fügner lay there knocked out, dead to the world.

Race officials scooped the crumpled and bleeding body into an ambulance and rushed to the hospital. A pall hung over the team. Those few fans who noticed the accident held their hands to their mouths. The rest barely noticed the siren as Ubbiali screamed to victory.

The Emergency doctors stabilized Fügner and assessed his injuries. They were catastrophic. That he fractured his skull was obvious, but they wouldn't know his prognosis until the swelling went down. That would take time.

When the medical staff discovered there wasn't enough blood for the transfusion, Walter volunteered to drive the 90 kilometres into Brussells to get more.

In his panic, he got hopelessly lost when he arrived in the city. Not knowing where to go, he parked the car and flagged down a taxi. The driver made a quick U-turn, darted up a side street, and dropped Walter off at the lab just around the corner.

To save money, he dismissed the taxi. He thought he could run back to the vehicle after collecting the blood; the distance was so short. However, when he emerged from the building, he was completely disoriented. He didn't know north from northwest. Exactly where should he turn? He panicked, running this way and that, frantic and lost.

Precious minutes later, when he spotted his car, parked exactly where he had left it, he was taken off guard. Surprised.

— What! You're here?

Shaking his head in disbelief, he fumbled for his keys. Still there. They hadn't fallen out. He sighed with relief and placed the insulated case with the blood on the floor beside him. He made the long trip back to Spa, flying low, the police mercifully catching speeders on another section of the road that afternoon.

The doctors gave Fügner a life-saving transfusion. One crisis averted, then onto the next and another, in a line stretching out to the crack of doom. It took Fügner months to recuperate and years to adapt to the new set of circumstances that now held him back. His life changed beyond belief.

Walter waited at the bedside until Frau Fügner arrived from Karl-Marx-Stadt. An experienced nurse, she became her husband's primary caregiver. She was a redoubtable advocate for his medical treatment, a woman of strength and vision. A good friend to have in times of trouble.

They started the long and arduous rebuilding of their life together. The old with its glory behind them, and the new with all its challenges ahead. But all was not lost. They were still standing on the tarmac, not laid low under it.

There was no renaming of the left curve to honour Fügner. They were grateful for what did not happen. They soldiered on.

Walter placed Fügner's battered helmet on a shelf in the shop as a reminder of what this *World Championship* campaign was costing them. He eventually appointed Fügner as Parts Manager for the *Rennkollektiv*, giving him a reason for getting out of bed every day.

The red zone may have become a pool of spilled blood, but it did not signal Fügner's Third Act. His story was not over. It was a hard new start, but he and Helga did not look back.

— *Dankbarkeit ist alles* (Gratitude is everything).

Up until Fügner's accident, the members of the *Rennkollektiv* thought they were invincible. After, it everything changed. While Fortune's wheel turned in their favour, they assumed their climb to the *World Championship* would be uncontested. The way would be clear, and they would suffer no harm.

However, they learned with Fügner that that was not to be the case.

Spa-Francorchamps taught them that although they were young and mighty, they could be brought low without warning. Destiny exacted its toll from everyone. Each paid the price. The *Rennkollektiv* was no exception, and the currency for competing in the *World Championship* was blood.

— Fortune's fool. With one turn, I am at the top. With another, the bottom. This is my destiny. I can do no other.

Walter pressed on.

Part Two

7

Unsere Schwester der Bäume
(Our Sister of the Trees)

Worn with care and heavy with woe, Walter straddled his newly found *DKW* motorcycle. Its rusted springs, desiccated rubber, torn gaskets, and cracked leather seat groaned in heady anticipation as he settled his whole weight down upon it.

— *Los geht's, altes Mädchen* (There you go, old girl). *Es ist lange her* (It's been a long time).

— *Sie sagen mir* (You're telling me). *Behandle mich einfach, wie eine Dame* (Just treat me like a lady). I am not your plaything. *Das ist alles, was ich frage* (That's all I ask).

—*Ja, wohl, gnädige Frau* (Yes, certainly, gracious Lady).

He bowed in humble obeisance.

— Now you're talking. My name is Dita, by the way.

— Parlo? Dita Parlo? *Meine Lieblingsschauspielerin* (My favourite actress), *als ich ein junger Mann war* (when I was a young man)?

— *Meine Namensschwester* (My namesake).

— I'm Kaaden. Walter Kaaden, at your service, Frau Dita.

— Herr Kaaden? *Sie können mich Dita nennen* (You may call me Dita). *Ich habe keinen Nachnamen* (I don't have a last name).

Walter laughed.

— In that case, you better call me *Onkel* Walter.

— As long as you stay where you belong. I may be an orphan without a family, but I have my boundaries and you need to respect them.

— Sounds good, Walter said, jiggling her gear shifter. I suspect that you are a crafty trickster who will challenge me to the outmost of my ability. But I am ready for whatever you throw my way.

— Where you go, I will go, and where you stay, I will stay. Your people will be my people, unless of course, I get a better offer.

— Then I'm your uncle, and Inge's your aunt. For as long as you choose. We will do the best we can for you.

Shortly after the war, Walter came upon Dita in the enchantment of a magical moment.

He and Inge were walking through the forest one late autumn Sunday afternoon when their young son Norbert caught a glimpse of some chrome glinting in the sunlight.

It drew him into the tangled underbrush.

— Mama! Papa! he yelled. The branches and twigs caught his clothes and scratched his arms and face. They tried desperately to slow him down. He couldn't move forward. He couldn't turn back. He was trapped in the underbrush.

His parents were white with fear. They ran pell-mell after their darling son, his little voice crying in the wilderness. They prayed he hadn't come upon an unexploded bomb.

— Please God, please God.

The words in their hearts couldn't escape their mouths. Earthbound, they ran without stopping, looking heavenward, praying for a miracle, yet expecting the worst. For as long as they could remember, God had ignored their anguish. Hadn't answered their prayers.

Norbert freed himself from the flaming red bush and kicked off his shoes to escape. He pulled away the canvas shroud and his parents saw the motorcycle he had found. They knelt beside him. Tears streamed down Inge's face as she wiggled her son's shoes back on and retied his laces.

— I am so unworthy, she cried. Thank you God for saving my boy.

Dita was in dire straits, and it broke their hearts. *Our Sister of the Trees*, they called her as they spent the rest of the afternoon lugging her back home. The parents pushed and pulled while Norbert balanced on the saddle.

— *Kleiner Junge* (Little boy), *bitte lass die Bremse in Ruhe* (please leave the brakes alone). *Fass sie nicht an* (Don't touch them). *Ich muss hier raus* (I need to get out of here). *Ich kann nicht länger hierbleiben.* (I can't stay here any longer). *Bitte hilf mir.* (Please help me).

Norbert smiled at her and gave her tank a rub.

She wept with relief. Like a genie set free, she had a world of dreams to offer her rescuers.

In his workshop at the back of the house, Walter drained the stale fuel from her tank and crankcase and changed the rank cloudy oil in her gearbox. He changed the tires, cleaned the carburetor, blew out the lines, and checked the magneto, points, and spark plug.

He kicked the starter while Dita sputtered, coughed, and gasped. His leg hurt, but she remained adamant. Her engine refused to fire.

Over the next few days, he cast out her demons and coaxed her back to life.

— *Ich fühle mich wie Lazarus* (I feel like Lazarus), d*er in ein Leichentuch gewickelt ist* (wrapped in a grave cloth), *und aus dem Grab hervorkommt* (coming forth from the tomb).

He hung the old tarp on a line out in the sun to dry. *The Shroud of Zschopau,* he thought as he contemplated the pattern of rips and stains in the canvas. Dita was crucified, suffered death, and was buried.

She descended into hell all the while hoping that her ascent into Heaven wouldn't be any time soon. She had miles to ride before she slept.

In the third year after the war, Dita rose from the dead. Walter cobbled her back together from bits and pieces he had found in forgotten bins, along with parts he was forced by necessity to fabricate himself. Innovative, he was resourceful and persistent.

Walter didn't quit.

A rat bike who no longer looked her best, Dita wasn't ready to go out performing in public. This wouldn't be a joy ride, she knew. They both had too much to lose.

Perhaps an empty street, an alley, or a slow country lane might do. Where they could idle slowly up to speed and take whatever time Walter needed to adjust this, tighten that, or loosen what needed loosening. He had a small bag of tools he could throw over his shoulder. He was a man prepared for whatever perplexity Dita threw his way.

She could tell that he was a handyman who knew his way around motorcycles. That she hid away in her heart. She liked how he cleaned his tools after he used them, and how he put them back where they belonged. They shone like newly polished chrome.

Babes in a manger, his wrenches were well-fathered.

St. Joseph the patron saint of engineers and workers blesses those who do soulful labour. Those who pay attention to the necessary things that each day requires are precious in God's sight. Can there be anything more heroic than being faithful to small things?

It's not easy being a stepfather and taking over where another has left off—fathering forth the unfathered. One day at a time. Being faithful in the here and now.

Dita would eventually start, but in her own time and on her own terms. She insisted right from the beginning that Walter was going to serve her.

He had better treat her right, or there'd be no going out or returning home. She demanded a relationship that was built upon dignity and respect.

None of the care or attention that Walter could give to Dita would remove from her soul the wartime ravages of fuel shortages, shoddy make-do odds and ends, haywire repairs, and utter abandonment she had endured. She had lost her trust, and it would take a long time for her to regain it.

Bitter and hurt, she was a motorcycle spurned by men who rode the Hell out of her. For all she knew, she could very well be on the road to another ravishment. The way ahead seemed bleak and hopeless. She was afraid.

The world of men had not been kind to her.

She had been on a *Via Dolorosa* on cobbled streets.

It chagrined her.

She could not believe that her salvation depended entirely on the hands of this desperate fellow. While she was grateful for his charity, she wondered what he expected in return.

What she had learned about life in this world is that nothing is ever free. She'd have to pay eventually.

But from his looks, she could tell that Walter was no ordinary man with a tool in his hand. An earthly saviour of broken-down motorcycles, he was a prophet in overalls who inhabited the in-between space where normal rules do not apply. He navigated through necessity, hardship, and deprivation, negotiating his way through one pitfall at a time.

Full of grace, he was a wise man who suffered fools gladly.

Diese Welt hat mehr zu bieten (This world has more to offer) *als man denkt* (than one thinks).

— It is a good thing, the prospect of getting back on the road again, Dita confessed, as she accepted Walter's absolution for her failings.

— *Das ist nicht deine Schuld, mein Kind* (It is not your fault, my child).

— And this just might be worth it, she said. After the burnouts, stalls, and races around the village square. After the litres of oil and jugs of fuel that spilled upon the workshop floor. It just might be worth it, after all.

Pulling down his helmet and tightening its strap, Walter zipped up his jacket and tucked in his scarf. With his gloves and goggles snugged on tight, he nudged Dita off her centre stand. He opened the fuel petcock and closed the choke. Pulling in the clutch, he shifted her into neutral. With a few deft kicks, he started her engine. She burbled to life, not with a roar, but with an indelicate belch. Blue smoke farted out of her tail pipe.

He eased the choke open.

— Oh, that feels good, Dita said. I need a good run to clear the crud out of my system.

— You are as ready as you'll ever be, Dita. There's fresh fuel in your crankcase and new oil in your gearbox. We'll go for a gentle ride through the village to lubricate your parts. As I run through the gears, I'll be listening for what's amiss. I won't hit 50 km/h, I promise. All I need is for you to sing soft and low.

He backed off on the throttle to prove his point.

— You'll need to be leisurely when we're on the road and back in the shop.

— You'll be fine. I'll go slowly. I promise.

Abandoned two-strokes are robust. Break them down. Oil each part. Clean the connections. Put them back together. Filled with divine spark, they'll come back to life. They are never a lost cause. That's a given.

Dita remembered the pair of Canadian airmen behind enemy lines. Brothers, it turned out. When they pulled the tarp off her, their eyes lit up. For the first time in a long time, hope grew in their hearts, hers too.

— That's Day-Caw-Vey, she corrected them, not Dee-Kay-Double-You.

They butchered her name but knew their motorcycles. They rolled her engine over a few times. She wasn't seized.

— She has spark, but her fuel is bad. We could drain her tank and steal some.

— And ride pillion down the road to perdition, Dita said. Maybe come to an untimely end?

That made them pause.

They decided it was safer for them to slink through the woods under the cover of darkness.

— Let's rest here a while.

Eventually, on a moonless night, they covered her up again.

— If you ever have the chance, come to southern Alberta. Steveville. Young Vern will be there. Us, too, if we survive. Our door is always open. Everyone knows *The Garage Mahal*. It has a snooker table. Just ask around. You'd be welcome.

She taught them that the German spoken to family and relatives, close friends, young children, pets, and in prayer to God was the language of love—not that god-awful French. While the formal and imperative in German are not to be taken lightly, there is grace in words that are spoken in tenderness.

Dita was a quick study. They taught her English: not American, British, or Canadian, but a hybrid. No one would ever mistake her for being a native speaker.

When Dita's engine warmed up, Walter opened the choke, and she settled down to a rough idle. He jiggled the throttle to keep the engine from dying. Tapping the shifter into first, he increased the rpm and the engine smoothed out. He eased out the clutch and took off down *Lindenweg* (Linden Way) towards *Rasmussenstraße* (Rasmussen Street). He headed into the country.

He needed a ride more than anything in this world.

She needed fiddling, taking apart, and cleaning.

Walter needed a carefree moment.

Dita needed loosening, putting back together, tightening, and lubricating. A good oil bath would do wonders for her soul.

Walter dreamed of a great ride with a homecoming fit for a prodigal.

— Yes, I will, yes, she purred.

Oil and petrol mixed with oxygen in her carburetor and pressurized in her crankcase, cooling her crankshaft, oiling her piston, rings, and cylinder wall, not to mention her head.

Attar of Petroil filled Walter's nostrils. The constriction around his chest lessened. He began to relax. He twisted the throttle and leaned into the next curve. He was about to enter the motorcyclist's sweetest dream, in which rider and machine are one with an open road ahead of them when Dita faltered.

Her engine hesitated. She coughed and lost power.

— Oh, I don't know, Dita stammered. Maybe this isn't such a good idea. My cylinder walls are dry, my float is jammed, and my spark is weak. Walter! You're going too fast. I can't do fifty. I am afraid.

— All right, Dita, all right, Walter said, and he backed off on her throttle. The engine settled down and ticked contentedly. A sweet bouquet of burning oil filled the air.

Walter breathed her in.

Smells like freedom. What a life. A man could only wish to ride a fine motorcycle in the morning. He'd get the victory. Soul full, pressed down and shaken together, brimming over. Life is a blessing. Walter couldn't get enough.

— Oh, that's better, Dita hummed. *Give me oil in my tank. Keep me from burning, burning, burning.* Give me oil in my tank, I pray.

8

Neue Anfänge
(New Beginnings)

Walter had heard that the Soviet-backed government in Berlin was shutting down all family businesses like his and Inge's. It didn't matter that they were building much-needed roof trusses for bomb-damaged buildings in Chemnitz (renamed Karl-Marx-Stadt in 1953) or that they employed thirty men during Germany's reconstruction.

— What'll our workers do? Inge asked. What about the people whose homes were destroyed? How much longer will they go without a place to live?

— The State will provide, Walter said. At least, I hope so. In any way, that's what they want us to believe.

— *Menschen brauchen Dächer über ihren Köpfen* (People need roofs over their heads), Inge said. *Das ist der Beginn der Weisheit* (That is the beginning of wisdom).

— Our company has always provided an essential service in a timely fashion. And we barely charge enough to cover our costs.

— I may have spent the war hiding under the stairs, Inge said. But I was not left entirely in the dark. Since the Russians invaded Berlin, I've had time to reflect on the changes that have since occurred. Moscow makes all the decisions, not their puppets. If you haven't completely clued in, Walter, let me set you straight. Our company is finished. If we're to stay in East Germany, we'll have to find another way to make a living.

— But what? Walter asked. This is our home. Unlike those *Flüchtlinge* (refugees) who make the headlines, we could never flee. We can't leave our parents behind.

— You'd be surprised what you'd do to keep alive.

— I know all about survival, Inge. I've done the unthinkable.

— Is that a confession?

— Just a matter of fact.

Walter was not as clueless as Inge implied. His resurrection of the old bike was not without intent. He had, indeed, looked to the future and saw that he needed an escape route in mind.

Long had the stale petroil in Dita's crankcase contaminated the ground where she had been abandoned. Long had the exhaust from her flared megaphone pipe fouled the air around Zschopau, and long had she known the history of the plant where she first found her being.

She knew that what once was could no longer be, and that which was coming could not be stopped.

The times were a-changing and they all needed retooling.

9

Jeden Sonntag
(On Every Sunday)

During the 1920s and 1930s, the factory that Jørgen Skafte Rasmussen founded in Zschopau was the largest motorcycle manufacturer in the world. In its heyday, 60,000 bikes a year rolled off its assembly line. That's over 160 a day. Then the Nazis converted it to an armament factory and set production quotas. When they conscripted the German workers to fight on the eastern front, they replaced them with slave labourers.

Before Dita's owner was forced to join the *Wehrmacht*, he hid her deep in the woods, under some brush for safekeeping. He never returned from the Battle of Stalingrad, and she languished alone, for years on end, winter, spring, summer, and fall.

She despaired over her owner's fate during the long siege and prayed for his safe return. She yearned for peace, all the while singing "Lilli Marleen," a song that Allied and Axis soldiers sang over long marches. It united both sides in their yearning to linger once again under the lamplight with their lovers. No matter what happened, Dita kept singing, year after year, calling for him to fill her tank with fresh fuel and set her free.

That the *Engländer* hadn't bombed the factory during the war remained a mystery to Dita and a relief to the citizens of Zschopau. Miraculously, it was still standing in March 1945 when the Russians overran eastern Germany. When the concentration camp guards abandoned their posts, the emaciated prisoners escaped the red zone and staggered west toward freedom and the prospect of new lives.

While those tired, poor, and huddled slaves got away with only the rags on their backs, Dita and the villagers stayed put. They kept their eyes open and worried about the dawning of the day ahead of them.

— *Es ist genug, dass jeder Tag seine eigene Plage habe* (Sufficient unto the day is the evil thereof).

No use thinking about tomorrow, they all thought, except for Dita.

— *Ich werde überleben* (I will survive). *Ich werde in die Zukunft schauen* (I will look to the future). *Dieses Mal werde ich auf das vorbereitet sein, was kommt* (This time, I will be prepared for what's coming).

After Germany's unconditional surrender, the Soviets stripped the factory of its assembly line components. They transported all the equipment and tools east of the Urals. They took along its senior personnel whose expertise they needed to refit the factory in its new location.

As part of Germany's war reparations, the Allies voided the patents on *DKW's RT 125*. Consequently, its elegant design and economical engine became the foundation for modern motorcycles all around the world.

— *Ich bin Jedes Motorrad* (I am Every Motorcycle), Dita said.

Based on the plans from Zschopau, the Soviets released the *Moskva M1A*, the Americans the single-cylinder *Harley Davidson 125*, and the British the *BSA Bantam*. Even the Japanese had a version that seven engineers from Nippon Gakki (today's Yamaha Corporation) developed, the YA-1.

— *Die Japaner werden mein Tod sein* (The Japanese will be the death of me). *Ich weiß es mit Sicherheit* (I know for sure), Dita prophesied.

At first, Walter tried to change the subject, but she refused to stop talking. She had been silent for so long that she would not shut up.

She had to speak her mind and he had to listen.

— What is rooted in war will find its way in blood. What is conceived in falsehood will burn to ash.

Passing through a series of curves, Walter rolled to a stop along the side of the road, lit a cigarette, and surveyed the valley below him. He knew that the older men sitting in the boardrooms in Berlin didn't have any imagination. They had an economic agenda that was stultifying. They lacked creativity, and they didn't pay up. They promised to fund the production of 5,000 new motorcycles, but would they deliver? He didn't think so.

Er braucht jedoch einen Job und hat sich entschieden (He needed a job and his mind was made up). *Er hatte keine Wahl* (He had no choice). Could he strike a bargain without selling his soul?

— Careful, Walter! Dita cautioned. Ideas like those will send you straight to *Ruschestraße* 103 (Stasi Headquarters). If we're going to conquer the world, you better watch your mouth. Those bastards can read minds.

— We'll need a lot more than what those bureaucrats in Berlin are willing to offer. Beautiful motorcycles are like women. *Teuer, aber jeden Pfennig wert* (Expensive but worth every penny).

— I see I have my work cut out for me, Dita sighed. *Darum seid klug wie die Schlangen* (Therefore, be as wise as serpents).

The people in Zschopau couldn't care less about the marquee on the side of the building, Walter said. *DKW*, *IFA*, or *Autounion*? What's the difference? They were sick of war. They barely survived the

Brown Shirts. Now they had to deal with the Stasi. They had enough of politics and grandiose dreams of world domination. Now, they wanted to get on with their lives. Eat, work, make love, and raise families. What more could they want?

— A fast motorcycle and winning races? Dita asked.

All week long, *Trümmerfrauen* (Rubble Women) shovelled debris from ruins, cleaned mortar from bricks, and cleared impassable streets while men erected walls, raised roofs, and repaired the Autobahn. They might never afford automobiles, but they could at least have decent roads for Sunday afternoon motorcycle races.

Nearly everyone in Saxony had a resurrected bike that idled its time in back sheds, waiting for Sundays when the worn-out, work-weary, and defeated could race them for fame and glory, earning the grudging respect of their neighbours and friends in villages down the road.

Their campaigns were on the highways and by-ways, not battlefields. They converted their weaponry into motorcycles and rode pell-mell to victory, damning defeat to Hell.

10

Des Knaben Wunsch
(The Boy's Wish)

Instead of handing in a resume of his education and experience, and thereby bringing to the fore questions the *DKW* factory management would prefer not to ask, and he'd rather not answer, Walter fixed up the old bike he pulled out of the bush and demonstrated on the road and during Sunday afternoon races all the mechanical wizardry he had to offer.

Every day, Walter rode Dita past the factory on his way to the construction site in Chemnitz.

— *Wenn ich ihnen nicht sagen kann* (If I can't tell them), *was ich getan habe* (what I've done), *kann ich ihnen zeigen* (I can show them), *was ich mit den wenigsten davon tun kann* (what I can do with the least of these).

— The least of these, Dita retorted. How dare you? After all I have been through! She wheezed, coughed, and then hesitated.

Walter's heart sank. He downshifted, turned around, and hurried back towards the shop. He had made another thoughtless remark and lost all the good will he had accumulated with her. When she refused to go any further, he pushed her the last 500 metres.

— That should teach you, she said.

Dita was, to put it mildly, in a pique. She admired Walter for being a gifted mechanic, but she resented her dependency upon him and lashed out.

— I prefer to be in charge of my own destiny. I've had more than enough of men and their tomfoolery. But you like the smell of my fuel, and I won't deny you the pleasure of giving me what I want.

Walter smiled and offered her a smoke.

Dita took a quick puff.

— *Ich mag Männer* (I'm fond of men) *mit Schmier in den Poren ihrer Haut* (with grease in the pores of their skin).

Walter tinkered with her ignition, filed her points, and tested her magneto. He adjusted her carburetor and changed the rubber seals, gaskets, and hoses. He rubbed the pit marks out of her chrome and adjusted her brakes. It took him all week to win back most of her heart, if not her undying faithfulness.

— I reserve the right to quit suddenly on any ride, especially when you are furthest from home. I will inconvenience you, so keep your fingers on the clutch lever. I'd hate for you to fly head and heels over these eye-catching handlebars if my engine seizes. I have my limits. You cannot ignore my red line.

Walter complied. He fidgeted and he pottered. Soon the old bike with its piddling 1.75 hp engine was racing down the road at a breathtaking 60 km/h.

When she buzzed even faster, people took notice of the crazy man on the little bike. Workers and managers leaned out of the factory windows and doorways. Their stopwatches clocked how quickly he was flying.

— Will wonders ever cease? They asked, as they laid down their bets.

— Not if I can help it, Dita said.

People in that motorcycle-mad, speed-crazy town were impressed. They could hardly believe that Walter Kaaden, the son of old Rasmussen's chauffeur, could coax that kind of performance out of such a motor. And a filthy two-stroker, at that!

Everyone knew that four-stroke engines were where the money was. That's what the public wanted to buy.

— Filthy? You're calling me filthy? Dita shook her head. You Friday night bathers!

She couldn't understand their obsession with those new-fangled four-strokes. Mixing a little benzine and oil, among other things, is all it takes to win a *World Championship*. Four-strokes are wallflowers compared to twos. Dita erupted in blue.

Des Knaben Wunsch (The Boy's Wish) *DKW* was more than a toy two-stroke engine that powered childhood dreams. It fired the fantasies of men and women who hungered for good times, freedom, and long rides down curved and sensuous roads.

Most of the villagers in Saxony were addicted to speed, singing, drinking, and dancing. They worked hard, but when the opportunity presented itself, they loved nothing more than a climactic roll on two wheels.

11

Glaube an kleine Dinge
(Faith in Small Things)

One Monday morning, Alfred Liebers, the recently appointed manager at *IFA* (*Industrieverband Fahrzeugbau*)—the *DKW* factory in Zschopau about to be renamed *Motorrad Zschopau*—stepped out onto the road to flag down the speeding Walter Kaaden.

Not paying attention to what lay ahead, Walter was pondering how to change out the megaphone exhaust pipe out for an expansion chamber and whether or not that would improve Dita's performance.

— It just has to, he said to himself. That Erich Wolf must be right.

When he looked up, he saw a man dive out of the way. At the last moment, Walter swerved into the ditch and tumbled off the bike.

— (*Dumm Kopf Walter*)! Dita groaned. *DKW!*

He wasn't hurt and the bike was only slightly damaged. His pride suffered a bruising, though.

Liebers stood up, likewise unscathed, and straightened his tie.

— Herr Kaaden, he said. Are you all right?

— Most certainly, Walter thumbed the *Kill* switch to On and dragged the now silent and fuming Dita back up onto the road. He closed her fuel petcock and put her up on her stand.

He flicked the *Kill* switch to Off.

—This bike's been through a lot worse.

— Idiot! Dita said, her engine smouldering. You should have concentrated on where you were going.

Liebers smiled.

— At least nobody was hurt.

— *Entschuldigung Sie, bitte* (Excuse me, please), Dita moaned as her tire rubbed against the front fender.

— I'll have one of my men straighten that out. He looked over his shoulder and beckoned to the tall one.

— Hackebeil!

He turned back to Walter.

— Do you have time to join me for a cup of coffee? I have a few questions. I'm Alfred Liebers, by the way.

Hackebeil wiped off his hands and hurried towards his boss.

— As a matter of fact, I could use a drink after that spill, Walter said.

— I bet you've pushed your bike further than I have ridden one, Liebers chuckled.

— I wouldn't doubt that Dita snorted as she gave Liebers the once over. *Deine Hände sind nicht schmutzig genug* (Your hands aren't dirty enough).

All bikes are divas. The tinier the engine, the narrower its power band, and the more difficult it is to master.

— Understanding small things is never easy, Liebers said. *Wer im Geringsten treu ist* (Who is faithful in the least), *der ist auch im Großen treu* (he is also faithful in the much).

Dita realized that Liebers did know a thing or two about insignificant matters of great importance.

She eyed the handsome Dieter Hackebeil, who hurried towards her, drinking him in, a lean John the Baptist in overalls, bit of a hooknose, curly black hair, olive complexion. Almost Italian. With an oily rag in his back pocket, he was quite the catch.

— Just don't lose your head, she warned herself. You could get into a tangle of trouble with that boy.

— You must seduce all engines with the right tools, terms of endearment, and exact mixture of fuel and oil, Walter continued. If you don't get everything just right, they're done with you.

— But can you make this squirt of a bike run any faster?

— Maybe. If I change the tailpipe for an expansion chamber.

— Those ugly things? They're a marketer's nightmare. You remember Kurt Kämpf? He earned Berlin's displeasure when he fitted them to the 1952 *IFA*. I warned him that no woman who respects her ears would be caught dead on a bike fitted with one of those.

Walter looked at him uncomprehendingly.

— Men may ride motorcycles, but women are the ones who determine household purchases. You must think of the person in control of the finances.

The thought that the consumer should be given some consideration in the design of a motorcycle had never entered Kaaden's mind before. For him, the only question worth asking was what could he do to improve engine output. Horsepower, speed, and reliability, not rider comfort or affordability, were his concerns.

— Women want true quality, Dita said. Not cosmetic beauty that is just skin deep. It's what is under the fairing that counts, not the colour of the paint job. Is the engine powerful enough? Will the bike stay the course? Can the rider repair it? How much does it cost?

Hackebeil looked to Liebers for instructions.

— Sir?

— That may be, Walter continued. However, in an engineer's world, form must follow function. Expansion chambers were never designed to muffle sound. Erich Wolf discovered that with some modification they could improve fuel efficiency and increase engine performance.

— Sir, Hackebeil tried to interrupt. Unnoticed, he remained standing and waiting, ready to serve if only he could get Herr Liebers' attention. A good and faithful man.

— A happy coincidence, Walter said. Kämpf was on the right track. His innovations could have taken *IFA* to the Winner's Circle.

— His rash outspoken manner made him too hot for the men in Berlin. They removed him.

— That may be, Dita mused. But I want to lean into a corner and blast out of its apex. I want to come first in every race I enter. *Ich bin kein Motorrad für alte Männer* (I am no motorcycle for old men). I love the young ones. They keep me in my prime.

She looked at Hackebeil. He was one she could inhale in a single draw and still be left begging for more.

Walter ignored her.

— By varying the shape and the length of the expansion chambers, we can tune the pipes short or long to maximize engine performance.

— That may be what's important for winning the *GP*. But what I'm really after is a reliable low-cost *Volksmaschine* (machine for the people) with interchangeable parts that people all over the world can afford to buy and repair themselves.

— I know from personal experience that nobody wants to ride a dud, Dita insisted. The only way to satisfy a rider is to have more fire in the pan.

— Expansion chambers speed bikes up.

— Now, how about that coffee? Liebers asked. I have a proposition you do not have the luxury of refusing. Oh, Hackebeil, there you are. Take Herr Kaaden's bike into the shop and repair that fender.

— Certainly, sir.

He turned to Dita.

— Young lady? Shall we?

Dita breathed out a huge sigh of relief. While he pushed her into the workshop, her tire yowled in pleasure against its fender.

— Yes, I will, yes, she wailed with the dawning of the age of this her new life.

12

Das Startertor
(The Starters Gate)

It was early morning, just after sunrise. Walter was unloading gear from the back of the factory's beat-up *DKW Kombi* van. He propped a couple crudely welded expansion chambers against a wall. The shop was cramped, dimly lit, and hardly more than a shed. It did not seem to be a workshop where innovative thinking and sound wave technology would transform old-school lacklustre two-engines into dynamos worth the reckoning.

On his regular early morning round through the factory, Liebers noticed that the newly hired Walter Kaaden was already there, toiling away alone.

He stood beside Dita.

— What's this? He asked, pointing to a pile of rusty saw blades.

— Worn out metal from my lumbermill, Walter said. The steel's too good to waste. I use it for fabricating whatever I need.

— You're certainly resourceful. How do you like the space we've given you?

— It's fine. I'm unloading my things before everyone starts work. Just getting a feel for my new job.

— That's good. You'll soon be putting in long days.

— I'll do whatever it takes.

— Making *IFA* competitive and racing the *Grand Prix* on the Continental Circuit will take more than hard work. You better be a miracle worker.

— What you call miracles, I call engineering. I believe in results that evolve from careful design and good workmanship.

— Luck is not to be sneered at. Often, circumstances mitigate against our best efforts. We could use a little serendipity around here.

— Luck comes to those who work for it.

— Do the best you can and hope it's sufficient. I suppose that's a matter of faith.

— Berlin wants you to sell racing engines that bring in foreign currency. As far as they're concerned, that's the most important part of your mandate. I want this factory to thrive for another fifty years.

— Survival in East Germany means finding out what Berlin wants.

— Moscow more likely, Dita said, piping up.

While she was a morning person, if you could call her that, she didn't need to engage with people as soon as she woke up. She needed some time and a shot of starter fluid before she could face her day.

These early birds were too chipper for her liking.

Liebers ignored her comment.

— Berlin wants to separate *IFA* into divisions with motorcycles being produced at the factory here in Zschopau. Trucks and automobiles at other sites.

— I suppose you'll replace the badge on my tank, Dita said. But I want more than pretty. I want unbeatable. Can you build a winner?

— That I can manage, Walter said. Foreigners will soon be stealing across the border to acquire our bikes.

— You'll have to produce maximum results with limited resources, Liebers cautioned. It's a political minefield here, and you cannot cross the line. Keep your wits about you.

— For all our sakes, Walter. Remember this is a red zone.

— Kurt Kämpf was brilliant, Liebers said. Unfortunately, he didn't know his place. He spoke his mind without considering the consequences.

Dita lit a cigarette, inhaled deeply, and smiled.

— These things taste better all the time. You may not be able to put a man on the moon, Walter, but you can win a motorcycle race. Just don't lose your soul. *Mephisto spielt nicht fair* (Mephisto does not play fairly).

— My faith is built on man's resourcefulness, Walter said. He has the potential to better himself. History does not look kindly on bastards. *Was ihr in der Finsternis saget* (what is whispered in darkness), *das wird man im Licht hören* (will be heard in the light).

— It's good to be a man full of conviction but you better leave room for openness and change. Difference. Understand that morality operates in a grey zone that is neither just black nor just white. The wisest navigate their way through extremes, setting a middling course to exit the curve in the fastest yet safest way possible.

— What I've learned in politics, Liebers said, is choose your words carefully. Express your opinions wisely. Align yourself with the right people. Do that which is necessary but remain full of tact and discretion.

Dieter Hackebeil entered the shop. He glanced up at the clock, surprised that someone else was in before him. He liked arriving first to ensure that everything was ready for the new day.

— Ah, there you are Hackebeil, Liebers said. I was wondering what took you so long. Remember him, Kaaden?

— The one who pulled the dent out of my fender the other day, Dita gushed. She nearly peed she was so happy.

— Of course, I remember. Thanks to you, Dita looks as good as new.

— Hackebeil's the best we have. He can solve any problem you throw at him. He even knows how to twist a wrench.

— *Es macht mir auch nichts aus* (I also don't mind), *meine Hände schmutzig zu machen* (getting my hands dirty). He gave Dita a quick glance. She smiled back.

Liebers hid his hands behind his back.

— Herr Hackebeil. Walter shook his hand in welcome. I'm sure there'll be plenty for you to do around here.

— I'm happy to work, Herr Kaaden. It's a privilege. And this fine machine? She has more potential than any of us can ask or imagine.

Dita smacked her lips. She loved the *Gewisses Etwas* (certain something) about this man who could push a two-stroke engine to its limit. That Hackebeil touched her soul.

Walter grabbed the last expansion chamber from the back of the van.

— This is a winning combination conceived in rocketry and executed on the track. Simplicity in design and careful engineering.

— I adore a man who can talk like that and twist a wrench. Now, I need to find someone to ride me to the fullest.

— We have some stiff obstacles to overcome, Walter replied, if we want to develop the world's fastest motorcycle.

— I may be small, Dita said, but I am mighty. I have ambitions beyond this toddling town.

Liebers turned to go.

— I'll let you three get on with your day. I need to phone Berlin.

13

Ohren, die nicht hören
(Ears that Do Not Hear)

— Who welded these monstrosities? Hackebeil asked as he scrutinized the line of expansion chambers. You're not thinking of fitting them to this gorgeous bike, are you? Look at her lines. She deserves better craftsmanship.

— It's fun toying around with Erich Wolf's ideas about these pipes, trying to figure them out. When they are properly tuned, they not only scavenge fuel, but they increase engine output. Bikes fitted with them go like stink. Nothing can beat them.

— The more fuel you can thrust in my cylinder, the more volatile my explosion, Dita said. I'll fly low and deliver a *World Championship.* That's a promise: my firstborn. Conceived in speed and delivered on the track.

— Sounds like natural supercharging to me, Hackebeil said, immediately grasping the implications of the piece of tail (pipe) in his hands.

— A clever way to get around the 1949 *FIM* (International Motorcycling Federation) ban on actual superchargers. The challenge, of course, is tuning the expansion chambers to the engine's rpm.

— The transformation of sound into music, Dita said. Pitch and rhythm, harmonics, and melody.

— The form that the sound of the exhaust makes in the rider's ear is an important aspect of racing motorcycles, Walter said. The riders know to shift gears when they hear the engine sing.

— It's the squalling of a newborn babe, signalling the beginning of life. The most hopeful sound in the world. Give me a rider who can make that kind of music, and I'll stand in the Winner's Circle. Preferably a jazz musician who improvises upon a theme, high tails it off into the unknown but returns in time for the accolades, applause, prize money, and final resolution. I want a man who always comes home.

— What I could use right now is an oscilloscope, Walter said. To measure sound. I need to analyze waves, amplitude, and frequency. The gases need to reach the exhaust port just before ignition, so that when the port opens, unspent fuel will be forced back into the cylinder. Properly timed, expansion chambers can double engine power. We already did this in the confined space of the V-2, but we can do it for a motorcycle?

— Like a church organ, Dita wondered. The higher the pitch, the higher the frequency, and the faster the sound wave?

— No, Hackebeil said. The speed of sound never changes. It is always a constant 343 metres per second, with some variation, depending on the temperature. The variable that can be changed, however, is the length of the pipe. The longer the pipe, the longer the distance the sound wave must travel. The slower the frequency of its return, the lower its pitch.

— The shorter the pipe, the shorter the distance, the faster the frequency, and the higher the pitch? Dita asked.

— Exactly, Walter said. By adjusting pipe length, we tune expansion chambers to an engine's ideal rpm.

— You can tell by the sound when the engine is running to its full capacity, Hackebeil said. According to the dynamometer, when this engine hits 6,000 rpm, it has reached its highest horsepower capacity. By fitting expansion chambers of varying lengths to it, we can either raise or lower its power. When it sings in tune, its output increases and we're off to the races.

— And go deaf in the process? Dita asked.

Walter and Hackebeil stared at her.

They did not have the ears to hear what she was saying.

14

Das raue Biest aus dem Osten
(The Rough Beast from the East)

Walter and Inge enjoyed a few minutes together in the workshop. While Walter sat on a stool, Inge leaned against Dita's new leather seat. Not Italian, but sturdy German, full grain and handstitched, ready for any rider who wanted to win races that count.

Inge took out a thermos and poured Walter some coffee. He wiped his hands on a cloth and took the cup from her.

— *Zimmerman ist ein guter Mensch* (Zimmerman is a good man).

Inge took an apple out of her bag and gave it a quick polish.

— Want some? She handed it to Walter.

— *Danke.* He took a big bite and gave it back.

— You finish it off. I've had my fill.

— If we don't do something about this new *ZPH* (Zimmerman Petruschke Henkel) motorcycle, we'll soon be out of work. Maybe I should talk to Hartmann. He might have an idea.

— I'm saying be careful. Kämpf's hot temper didn't help him in the job you've now landed.

Walter shrugged.

— It's no wonder Zimmerman's bikes are so quick, Dita said. That Petruschke is the best rider in East Germany, and Henkel is a skilled mechanic. He knows how to get motorcycles into racing form.

— They beat us on the track every time.

— Not every time, Walter said. When they have a breakdown. That's when we win.

— So, what are you going to do about it? Inge asked.

Well versed in the ways of men, she knew how to get Walter to do what she wanted. Get him to think her idea was his. Ask loaded questions that draw him to her way of thinking. Not once in his marriage did Walter ever clue into what she was doing. Her questions full of innocence and wonder had their desired effect. Walter blissfully did whatever she wanted. Every time. He was a good man.

— Make Dita the most durable racing machine in the world. Design an engine that'll run longer than anything else on the track.

— That and hope Hartmann has our best interests in mind. He says he has everything under control. He's pushing *ZPH* out of business.

— Pardon?

— He's transferring Zimmerman to watersport.

— And where does it leave us?

— In Hartmann's favour, as long as we're useful to him.

— But what about Petruschke? Dita asked. Where does he fit in?

— Hartmann will put him back on the *Rennkollektiv* roster, Inge said.

— This is too much!

— But it might be our best option, Inge said. That old Communist has too many friends in the Party to cross.

— Hold your nose and do what you have to?

— And if we don't?

— Lose everything, Inge said.

— What about Dieter Henkel? What'll happen to him?

— With his skills, he won't have any difficulty finding work. East or West.

— Do you think he'd defect?

— The border's open. Thousands are frantic to leave before Berlin tightens its controls.

— Soon those who want to leave will have to risk life and limb.

— Do what you're told. Raise no ire. We're here for the duration. If we leave, we lose everything.

— Besides, who'd hire me in the west? I built rockets for the Nazis.

— Maybe join von Braun?

— I'm not interested. There's been enough killing. I want a better life. Racing the world's fastest motorcycle. That's my dream. Flying low.

— Do that and maybe keep your job, Inge said. Talk to Hartmann. You don't want to fail. It's a long night when you're on the losing side.

Walter threw the apple core into the garbage. His eyes opened to the world around him. Sometimes, there is such a thing as too much knowledge.

Hackebeil finished working on a motorcycle at the far end of the shop. He walked over and joined them, polishing a 10mm wrench, his weapon of choice.

— Hungry? Inge asked.

— *Immer,* Frau Kaaden, he replied. (Always.)

She poured him a coffee and handed him a bun.

— We were never intended to live on bread alone.

— *Lecker* (Delicious)! The butter and jam are heavenly.

— What do you think? Walter asked Hackebeil. Of us asking Hartmann for more funding?

Hackebeil sipped his coffee before answering.

— With the *Sportkommissar* (sports commissioner) on our side, anything is possible. Pay him a visit but take Dita with you. She can be very persuasive.

Inge tidied up the lunch things from the counter.

— Hartmann isn't the enemy, she said. I could teach him a thing or two. But he'd need to listen.

— Pardon? Walter asked.

— What did she say?

— I'm not sure.

15

Das Motorrad im Zimmer
(The Motorcycle in the Room)

Walter managed to deliver Dita to the Sports Commissioner's office in Berlin without anything untoward happening. The trip down the elevator was the hardest part of the journey. The old men in suits and uniforms and young women in tight skirts and low-cut blouses were loath to share their space with such a fine racing machine.

— She smells of oil and petrol, they complained, giving her the cold shoulder.

Dita kept her mouth shut but thought they all reeked of body odour, stale aftershave, cheap perfume, and tobacco. For once in her life, she decided not to exacerbate the situation by speaking her mind.

Walter jockeyed her into the elevator.

— *Entschuldigen Sie, bitte* (Excuse me, please).

Those who could moved further back into the corners of the elevator, while those who couldn't stepped out and waited for the next car going down into the sub-basement. Alfred Hartmann may have been the lynchpin in Zschopau, but in Berlin, he was one of the smaller cogs in its vast bureaucracy. He drew headlines in the sport section but avoided the front pages as much as possible. That kind of exposure was never good.

Dita and her fellow passengers descended into the deepest darkest recesses of the building. No suits or uniforms were wrinkled and most importantly, no hose for those women who had connections to the West was snagged.

To reduce the tension, Dita decided to flirt the whole way down. Despite the initial antagonism everyone felt towards her, she was on a first-name basis with one and all by the time the elevator reached the sub-basement floor. They warmed to her and ended up loving her with a passionate intensity.

Why not respond to unkindness with kindness? Dita thought to herself. I am, after all, in the entertainment business. These people will soon be my fans. By smiling, I've made sure that they will never forget me.

With a fair amount of rocking back and forth and a good-natured jostling with Dita's new-found Communist sympathizers, Walter rolled her out of the elevator, down the hall, and into the boardroom without scuffing the walls, dinging the doors, or marring the furniture. He placed her front and centre, so that Hartmann and the committee members could see her with their own eyes before dismissing out of hand his request for more funding.

— Herr Hartmann, comrades. This is the new *IFA 125* with a three-speed gearbox. She's our latest offering and quite the beauty in the buff. On the track, of course, she'll be covered with a full fairing.

With her bounty on display, Dita acknowledged the room full of men with a drop of glistening gearbox oil splatting down on the gleaming hardwood.

I may not be a British trollop, Dita thought. But at least I can act like a sexy beast.

— How can something this small go that fast?

Through Walter's wizardry, Dita thought. The magic of physics and mechanical processes at 6,000 rpm. It's in the transformation of a reciprocating vertical action into the rotational motion of the crankshaft. A horizontal means for getting ahead.

— We keep the weight down. That's why we need high-grade aluminum.

— It's fine-looking, one of the committee members....

— But that ugly exhaust pipe, another interrupted.

— It's an expansion chamber, *Schatzi.* An exquisitely tuned instrument. Organists measure their sound in terms of metres and centimetres. The longer the deeper, the shorter the higher. Mine is measured in micro millimetres.

The shock wave must return to the cylinder as the piston hits top dead centre. When that happens, I can reach a high C.

— Like Wagner's Brunnhilde? Hartmann asked.

— More like a fiery hornet, Walter replied.

— A song born in immolation, Dita said hotly. A cry from the soul.

— This bike is designed to win races, Walter said. We need the finest quality steel for her piston rings, aluminum for her cylinder walls, proper racing tires, modern brakes, and racing shocks to stabilize her chassis.

— How about a dedicated test track, not just a temporarily cordoned-off part of the Autobahn, a wind tunnel, and a new dynamometer to measure engine performance? Dita asked. Maybe even a state-of-the-art oscilloscope? Our competitors have the latest equipment and we have baling wire.

— Seems like a complete waste, one comrade complained to another. The country can't afford such luxury items right now.

— Luxury? Dita protested. You think my spare design is luxurious? Walter has worked miracles to get my weight down to a scant seventy kilos.

— Good governance requires well-stocked shelves when its citizens need groceries. Societies fall apart when there is no food or salt.

— East Germans dream about fast motorcycles when they go to and from work.

— We need construction equipment, farm tractors and ploughs, not consumer goods.

— Yes, day-long queues are soul-destroying, Dita admitted. We need staples to survive, but we also need hope. At Sunday races, fast bikes give people the freedom they do not have during the week. Speed brings them the satisfaction they all crave.

— People need to food to live. Wasteful extravagance does not feed empty mouths.

— Sunday afternoon motorcycle races are a cure for the soul. Creation through recreation. Motorcycling brings hope.

— We are struggling against global forces and East Germans need to stand as one, Hartmann said. We need heroes whom the people can adore and idolize. Hopefully, someone young and beautiful for the headlines.

16

Unter der Decke
(Under the Covers)

With the buzz of motorcycles gnarling around Sachsenring, Dita, Walter, and Alfred Hartmann cheered the *MZ* riders on. While it was good to see the entire team on the track at the same time, Walter knew that there wasn't a superstar among them. Brehme, Fügner, Haase, and Musiol were the fastest racers in East Germany, but they weren't good enough to win on the international stage. He had to keep looking.

Hartmann took a packet of smokes out of his pocket and offered one to Walter.

— Hey! Dita said. What about me?

Hartmann handed the pack to Dita, but she declined in a huff.

— Trying to kill me?

— If we can't beat our countrymen in competitions here in East Germany, how do we expect to win on the Continental Circus? Walter asked.

— It's sometimes the things you do off the track that have implications on the track, Hartmann replied.

— But we don't have a chance against the likes of Geoff Duke and Umberto Masetti.

— It's their budgets, Dita said. The resources *Norton, Gilera,* and *MV Agusta* have for their racing departments are formidable. No wonder we can't compete against them.

— You have to make do; Hartmann insisted. That's why we appointed you. You're a resourceful engineer.

— And if I can't?

— Moscow has guns pointed at our heads. You, me, Dita, our families. If we don't win, Berlin will pull the trigger.

— You better pick your battles and concentrate on winning a skirmish or two, Dita said. That'll hold the wolves off.

— Like focussing on smaller displacement engines? Walter asked. Forgetting about the 350s and 500s? Our 125 now delivers 13.5 horsepower at 9,500 rpm. With that, we can reach 151 km/h. There could be more.

— That's how underdogs win battles, Dita said. Leave the big guns alone.

— How do we gauge our strengths and assess our weakness? Hartmann asked. What exactly is the problem with the 125?

— The transmission, without a doubt. It's yesterday's gearbox. I don't think our new four will cut it.

— Then get to work, Dita said. Your mastery of two-strokes and expansion chambers is legendary. If anyone knows how to shift gears, you do.

Walter couldn't argue. He took a long drag on his cigarette and watched Horst Fügner on an *MZ* 125 trying to keep up with the Spaniard Marcelo Cama on a *Montesa.*

Suddenly, the small Spanish bike lost its speed and Fügner shot ahead. Cama rolled to a stop and let out the clutch. He leaned the bike against a lamp post and stormed off. Her engine seized, the rider ablaze, and his dream of another checkered flag up in thick black oily smoke. She was a motorcycle on a road to nowhere.

— What do you think happened? Dita asked.

Walter shook his head.

— Not sure. She has a beautiful voice, though. I love it when motorcycles sing their hearts out.

— Check out what's under her fairing, Dita suggested. Maybe give her shifter a wiggle. See how many gears she has. It might reveal why you can't keep the lead.

Walter tried to ignore her.

— I want to win the *Grand Prix* through hard work and honesty, not trickery. I refuse to be underhanded in my dealings. I have my good name to consider.

— Is that all that is holding you back? Hartmann asked. You better get a move on. Being a stickler about fair play won't gain you any favours back in Berlin. Or here on the track. The Spaniards have abandoned her. There's no one around. Give that Senorita a look. See what makes her fly.

— We're using last year's three-speed gearbox. That's the issue. The new four-speed we've been working on isn't ready.

— Look under her covers. For God's sake!

— But ask nicely, Dita said. I'm sure she won't mind. We motorcycles are partial to those who are interested in what makes us tick. But don't lollygag!

— If you've gotta cross the line, Hartmann said. Cross the line! International recognition is what Berlin is after. Get that and the world is ours. If you hesitate, we'll be in the crosshairs.

— Don't mess with Berlin!

— Dita's right. Besides, you have Norbert to consider, Hartmann added. His future is at stake.

— I'm an engineer. I use mathematics to solve my problems. I don't steal other people's work. I have enough ideas of my own.

— When they'd steal yours in a fraction of a second? Someone is waiting to make a fool of you. Spying isn't just about politics and global affairs. Industrial espionage is a thing. You have knowledge everyone wants. They're willing to pay for it, too.

— Walter, you need to check Cama's bike. What does she have that I don't?

— Dustbin fairings may be aerodynamic, but they cover up the interesting bits.

— Then give her a look, Dita said. She might even relish your attention.

— This goes against my better nature, Walter said.

— You need to do what needs to be done before we are undone, Hartmann said. Berlin has its eye on us. This is war. Do your fucking duty or we'll get shot.

— If it were done when 'tis done, then 'twere well / It were done quickly.

— Indeed, if it were done, when 'tis done. But I know it won't be. Repercussions no matter how insignificant are unstoppable. They radiate outwards. There's no end to the harm they will do. A shock wave of consequences.

Walter nodded and lit another cigarette. He pulled his cap over his eyes and wandered over to the tiny bike, forlorn against the lamp post.

— *Hola, Liebling,* (Hello, Darling) *¿Qué tal* (how's it going)? Walter asked, his Spanish more limited than his English. He approached her from the left-hand side. Are you okay?

— *Muy bien* (Very good), she answered, irritated in the hot sun, her insides burned to a crisp.

— Do you mind if I see what's going on?

— I don't but my team might.

Walter looked over his shoulder to see an armada of Spaniards hauling in the wind towards him. He hoped a sudden gust of wind would blow them hopelessly off course.

— Your transmission? He knelt beside her, pulled in the clutch, and moved the shifter. It clicked as the gears moved out of neutral and into position. One down and five up.

— Six speeds. Well, I'll be damned.

He put her back into neutral.

— And we're running three. No wonder we're losing to you.

He loosened her fuel cap and gave her tank a quick polish.

— *¿Se van tan pronto* (Leaving so soon)?

— Come and see me sometime. We could do great things together.

— A quick glance ahead is sometimes all you need to know what needs to be done.

17

Träume und Visionen
(Dreams and Visions)

The door to the workshop burst open. Norbert flew in. He was still in his school clothes and frantic.

— Dita! He yelled.

— Ahh, there you are, my boy.

He ran over to her, gave her throttle an affectionate twist, and breathed in the perfume she exuded.

Oil and gasoline, she reminded him of his Papa.

Walter kissed his son's head.

— Learn something new at school today?

— That I love Dita best.

Stressed and exhausted, Inge stormed in, carrying her husband's midday meal, *Kartoffeln und gemischter Salat* (potatoes mixed with shredded raw vegetables and lettuce).

— Leave that bike alone, she said. It's not a toy.

— I wouldn't be too sure about that, Dita said.

Inge's spine stiffened. She had ears to hear but not the patience to tolerate any more of his back talk. She had enough. Besides, she resented Dita's pull on her family.

Walter hugged his boy.

Inge turned towards Norbert.

— Don't get into anything you shouldn't.

— *Ja, Mama.*

Walter let Norbert go and took the basket from her.

— Thanks, dear. He carried it to the table. He washed his hands and began to eat.

— Norbert, what are you doing? Inge asked.

— Just polishing Dita, Mum.

— What is she filling your mind with?

— *Nichts, Mama* (Nothing, Mum). She's just a bike.

Dita arched her eyebrow. *Tante* Inge was in a pique over something, and Dita knew best to leave her alone.

— Walter? Inge asked.

— Dreams *und* visions, he answered. *Eure alten Leute sollten Träume haben* (Your old people should have dreams), *und eure jungen Leute sollten Visionen sehen,* (and your young people should see

52

visions). That's what Dita offers East Germans. Broken-hearted hope in a verdant yet dreary land.

Inge looked at the finely wrought motorcycle and shook her head.

— It's like you're never home.

— I'm busy here. Berlin wants us to win, and I need to develop a new transmission. I thought I had something with the four, but now the competition is running sixes.

— First, you spend all your days getting the workshop organized. Then you're tied up until midnight, perfecting those bloody expansion chambers. Now you're fussing in the early hours over gear boxes. What's next?

— We start at St. Wendel in Saarland. Then it's the Continental Circus all over Europe. With Monza on 1 September, we don't expect to win, place, or show, but just be there and introduce ourselves to the world. Then next year it's Montjuïc, Hockenheimring, Charade, Isle of Man, Assen, Spa-Francorchamps, Sachsenring, Dundrod, Monza, Kristianstad, and Buenos Aires. The world is ours for the taking. 1961 will be an auspicious year for us.

Inge looked back at her son.

— Norbert, she called. *Mach dir nicht die Hände schmutzig* (Don't get your hands dirty).

He ignored her and continued to polish Dita's front wheel.

— That's my boy, Dita purred.

— I can almost see my reflection in her chrome, he yelled back.

— Walter, I can't go on like this, Inge said. You're missing Norbert's growing up years. He won't be a boy for much longer. You spend far more time with Dita than you do with me. I survived the war without you because we had no choice. Now you're about to travel all over Europe. With no end in sight.

— Do you think that I have any say? Walter picked at his food. I'm just a pawn.

— The Continental Circus is a caravansary, Dita said. Except wins follow design not serendipity. Without Walter, *MZ* would collapse faster than a wall in the winds of change.

— Well, you better manage your team more effectively, Inge said. Now that you have good men working for you. Let them do their jobs. Micromanaging will be the death of our marriage. You don't need to attend all the races. Oversee the stars at the *World Championships*, maybe, but, for God's sake, let others take over the second-tier races. Maybe one of the old-timers?

— *Tante* Inge has a point. Listen to her.

Walter knew he had to make some adjustments to the way he was doing things, or there wouldn't be any dessert after his meal.

Part Three

18

Ein kleines Stück Magie
(A Little Piece of Magic)

— *Gott im Himmel,* (God in Heaven) *Onkel!* Who is that bombshell over there? Dita asked as he handed her a cigarette. They stood out in the sun with Hartmann, watching the comings and goings from the main office.

— Oh, don't you know her? Hartmann asked. That's Gerda Bastian, Degner's girl.

— Degner?

— You know, Bernhard Petruschke's young friend, Walter said. When Berlin forced the closure of the East German racing teams competing against us, Petrus sold Degner his new *ZPH* motorcycle for a song.

— Deg's been racing as a privateer, Hartmann said.

— The boy from Potsdam? The apprentice magician who's been giving us such a hard time?

— Exactly.

— You didn't tell me that you were trying to recruit him. Dita cuffed Walter on the shoulder.

— I wasn't sure Berlin would let us keep him. Besides, I thought that you knew everything.

— *Ich bin vielleicht das einzige Stück Magie in deinem Leben* (I may be the one piece of pure magic in your life), Walter Kaaden. *Aber ich bin nicht allwissend* (But I'm not omniscient).

— Could have fooled me.

— We've offered the lad a contract, Hartmann said. I confess. He's negotiated a side deal for his fiancée. It took time to work out the details.

— They are quite the package, aren't they? I mean what with his looks and her legs; they could open any door. You old goats!

— Form always follows function, Hartmann intoned, straightening his tie. We hire according to merit, not looks or political connection.

Dita's eyes turned to the old Communist Petrus as he joined the young *MZ* racers for smokes.

— And you're certain about that?

— All right, I confess. You caught me. It's her relationship with Degner that shooed her in. She's a woman none of us could refuse.

— And Petrus brought in Degner. Goes to prove it's who you know that counts.

— And luck, Walter added. No matter how hard you work, a happy accident in your favour goes a long way. It's never just who you know; or how you perform; or what you do. It's being present and taking advantage of an opportunity that arises out of nowhere.

— *Und es wird viel Glück geben* (And there will be great luck) / *Von kleinen Kindern, die ihr Bestes geben* (For little kids who do their best), Dita said, reciting *Struwwelpeter,* (Heinrich Hoffman's *Shaggy Peter* stories about the terrible consequences of misbehaving).

— Degner's too good a prospect for us to pass up. He's a fine racer. But what about her? Dita asked. What does *Fräulein* Bastian have to offer the *Rennkollektiv?*

— Emotional support and comfort at home.

— As a domestique? Dita asked.

— As a safety anchor, Hartmann said. As a shackle to keep her husband returning to his home in East Germany.

— She will add quite the look to our lacklustre brand.

— Marketing isn't our strong point.

— The West has shown time and time again that sex appeal sells.

— That's the gutter press for you, Walter said.

— No. That's human nature. We all want what's attractive.

— The secret to our success is combining *ZPH*'s crankshaft-powered rotary valve with our tuned expansion chambers, Walter said. Not the shade of blue in the paint, or the badge on the tank.

— People crave beauty they cannot have and performance they'll never attain, Dita replied. Don't forget that.

— Short skirts, long legs, and podium finishes are all part of a winning package, Hartmann said.

— Spoken like a politician. Walter shook his head in disgust.

— So? Staying in power is all that matters.

— What *MZ* needs more than anything is a gorgeous young couple, Dita said. Could you imagine the impact of a photo with Ernst Degner and Gerda Bastian on the cover of *Neue Berliner Illustrierte* (*New Berlin Illustrated*)?

— She's right, Walter. You and I both know it. The camera will eat Gerda and Degner up. We need their star power to reach into the homes of all the citizens of East Germany. They'll show the world how superior East Germany is to life in the West. No one will want to leave.

— Especially when those two marry and start having babies. East Germans will follow their every move. They'll be royalty.

19

Die Löwengrube
(The Lion's Den)

— Hey, *Onkel!* Dita screamed. Did you see Lottes on that *MV?* Cut our Deg right off. Squeezed past Petrus. The bastard!

— Karl Lottes is a good rider. We have a long history of him beating us. Petrus should have known better.

— Well, I think he's a prick. Karl Lottes *aus* (from) Marburg riding for *MV Agusta* when he should be riding for us.

— He's a good German. Hartmann laughed. Chasing after the money.

— But those fat-cat Italians, Dita swore. They bought him.

— You wouldn't say that if he were pressing down into your saddle.

— Oh, shut up, Alfred. Can't you see I'm serious? God, sometimes you make me so mad!

— All I know is that we're on his tail. For once, we aren't falling behind.

— But this is still Germany. See this map? St. Wendel isn't exactly the Lion's Den.

— I wouldn't know about that, Walter interrupted. All the big names are here, and we're keeping up.

— Come on, Walter! A podium finish at the *GP* is still a long way off.

— But it's no longer outside the realm of possibility.

— That I have a hard time believing, Dita said, seeing my Ernst getting trounced like this.

She slumped down on her centre stand.

— First names, Dita? You really should show more respect for the racers. They aren't all your lovers.

— Let me tell you *Sonnenschein* the men I choose are electrifying.

— What did you say? Hartmann asked.

— There needs to be some mutual attraction. When younger men flirt, I'm flattered. When old farts make the first move, I'm annoyed. Hands off until I invite you.

— Huh? Walter asked.

— Don't be upset, uncle. You brought me back from the grave and I love you according to my bond, nothing more.

She shifted her well-turned and sensuous forks towards Alfred.

— You, on the other hand, have no equal. You're the only man who can truly satisfy my needs. Just give me what I want whenever I ask. I love you more than words can convey.

— We all have secrets, Hartmann replied. I'm not in this just for the fun, you know. I want you and me to go places. You're my ticket to the world. Take me where I want to go, and all this is yours for the asking.

He pointed to a map of the world hanging on the wall.

— Geneva, London, Milano, New York. But Berlin first needs to stake its claim, and the sooner, the better. Don't you forget that! We could lose everything.

— Then you better get us more funding, Walter said. *Es braucht Gold, um Gold zu gewinnen* (It takes gold to win gold).

— Don't hold your breath, Dita said. Berlin has other priorities.

— Like what?

— Competing in the Olympics, Hartmann boasted. That's where the real treasure is.

— *Bitte* (Pardon)? How can that be? The Olympics? And you think that I'm a dreamer? You should hear yourself. We weren't allowed to participate in London's 1948 Austerity Games. We still don't have a chance. Not for a long time, anyway.

— You could tell whose side the *IOC* was on in 1952, Dita said. West Germany participated in the Helsinki games, but not us. Athletes are little more than playthings to the gods. Sport is a geo-political tool.

— Will East German teams ever wear their own uniforms and fly their own flag? Walter asked. Or hear their own national anthem?

— Not anytime soon, I'm afraid, Hartmann said.

— But we still won't have a chance, will we? Dita asked. With the *IOC's* refusal to recognize us.

— That remains to be seen. Our athletes are among the best in the world. Soon they'll have to.

— How can that be? Walter asked. Really. We're a country of 17 million. West Germany has three times that. How can we compete? We don't have the gene pool.

— Don't be so naive. Alfred has other ways and means to enhance athletic performance.

— Pardon?

— Once we start winning medals, the truth will come out, Hartmann said. East German youth are superior to those from the West. That I can guarantee.

— In the meantime? While we wait for these kids to advance through our Olympic training programs?

That'll take too long. *Wir müssen irgend etwas tun* (We have to do something), *und das in der ersten Hitze* (and in the first heat).

— *FIM* has no restrictions that I know of against East Germany, Walter said. Six races a year. Sometimes ten. Year in and year out. All over Europe. With crowds of 200,000 and more. A poor man's sport, maybe. But very popular among the working class.

— It's one they can afford to support.

20

Die Insel Man
(The Isle of Man)
June 1961

Union Jacks snapped in the breeze. Dita and a handsomely dressed Japanese gentleman sat on a patio overlooking the quay at Douglas on the Isle of Man.

— Everything went swimmingly, Dita laughed. That is, until we tried to board the ferry. The new transport truck Berlin gave us was too big. We're East Germans. We didn't know the ferry was so small. We had to offload the essentials and stow them on the bus. Then we walked on as foot passengers.

— Paul Petry suggested that I talk to you, Jimmy Matsumiya said.

— About what?

— Ernst Degner. Petry mentioned that he is unsatisfied with the compensation he's receiving from *MZ*.

— He's our star. I don't know what he is complaining about. The rest of the team is paid far less. You should see the apartment in Karl-Marx-Stadt (renamed Chemnitz in 1990) that the State gave him and Gerda as a wedding gift. The nation adores those two.

— Mr. Suzuki has deep pockets and pays his riders handsomely, if he gets good value in return.

— Money's important to Ernst, but so's winning. Losing's not part of his nature. Those *Colledas* of yours don't have a chance.

She took a sip of the Dirty Martini in front of her and made a wry face.

— People like this?

She put the glass down and tightened the cap on her fuel tank.

She luxuriated in the warm sun, sheltered from the cool breeze that blew in from the Irish Sea.

Matsumiya swirled the ice cube in his dram of single malt. An elegant and sophisticated Oxford accent softened his Japanese-tinged English. Hers was primitive and rough, off-kilter, unmistakably German, and filled with the pain of bad gas, heat-warped rings, and missed gear shifts on hard turns into tight curves. It assaulted the ears.

She was smart and intelligent. Her thoughts were clear and to the point. Only her words were awry, lurching sideways out of her mouth. Like a Canadian trying to speak German.

— How'd you learn your English?

— My parents wanted to prepare us. In case we lost the war. It turns out they were right. Where'd you learn yours?

— A pair of pilots. From western Canada. They didn't know south from southwest. They found me in the bush and spent days trying to get my engine started. They hoped to ride me all the way to Switzerland but came to their senses when they realized that they would be a bull's eye fit for target practice. Two men riding the wrong way away from the fighting? What could go wrong?

— Survival is often a matter of sober second thought. A situation arises, then we scramble. Precaution is a luxury we're deprived of in battle.

— They were good soldiers who planned their best lines of defence before they advanced.

— That's why I'm here, not blown apart. War taught me to do my job and to keep my head low. I came to Oxford to study English, and *Suzuki* hired me to look out for their interests.

— Lately, I've been conjugating verbs with Alan Shepherd. Language learning is so much more fun when you're in someone's arms.

— What does his wife say?

— When she married him, she knew that she would never be his one and only. The only thing he cares about is racing and fiddling with machines that'll get him to the podium. He knows how to advance my spark. Of that, there is no denying.

— After the *RAF* firestorms of Darmstadt, Dresden, Hamburg, and Kassel, Walter still loves the English? How is that possible?

— When they can make a profit, British companies are always quick to forgive and forget. If we need something, we ask, and they find a way to get it to us.

— With all that happened in the war, your countries are still close? Matsumiya shook his head.

— We've been friends for generations. Look at the Royal Family. They were once German. Now they fit right in. Pure English.

— You should have seen us when we first arrived in Douglas, Matsumiya laughed. Unwelcome and out of place. There's still a lot of animosity for the Japanese here.

— I'm not surprised after Hong Kong.

— In war, there are no innocent parties. In peace, we need to live in harmony. But it's mostly a hit and miss process. Time may eventually heal wounds but not the scars. They linger for a lifetime.

Grand words like appeasement, conciliation, and pacification are meaningless by themselves. Small acts of kindness done in the everyday are the only way to bring reconciliation to our world. What goes around comes around. Eventually.

— In the meantime?

— We win motorcycle races.

— I drove Mr. Suzuki and Mr. Maruyama around Snaefell. Do you know what surprised us the most?

— The topography?

— No. We expected mountains. What got us? The roads. They're covered in tarmac. Back home we race on dirt and gravel.

Matsumiya adjusted the brim on his Panama hat and sipped his smoky *Laphroaig*.

Dita smiled.

— I bet the full Manx breakfast knocked you for a loop.

— You're not kidding. Two eggs, sausage, and beans followed by something inedible. After all my time here, I'm still not used to it. We order fish and chips and eat the fish. Toss the rest. It's the most palatable thing they serve in Britain.

Matsumiya glanced at his Rolex.

— It's almost time to watch our boys win.

— You mean, see *MZ* win and *Suzuki* lose? Your *Colledas* are pathetic.

— These are early days. *Suzuki* is about to take on the world.

Dita pushed her drink away while Matsumiya paid the bill.

— Just leave Ernst alone. He has a family, you know.

But Matsumiya couldn't care less.

He jumped on Dita, twisted her throttle, and rode her hard to the finish line.

21

Auf zum Gemetzel
(To the Slaughter)

To no one's surprise, least of all to the members of the *Rennkollektiv*, *MZ* performed abysmally at their first Isle of Man *Tourist Trophy*. The carbs weren't calibrated to the altitude, or the ignition to the fuel. Just getting to the island in one piece was a victory for that unkempt ragtag of a team.

Walter tried to encourage them.

— *Wir sind hier für die Erfahrung* (We are here for the experience). *Nächstes Jahr werden wir unter die ersten drei kommen* (Next year, we'll finish in the top three).

Degner, angry as Hell at the idiots around him, needed time alone.

With Hartmann's permission, he wandered through Douglas, trying to clear his head. He had a few British pounds to spend, not much he knew, but more than the other members of the *Rennkollektiv*. Enough to get some pantyhose for Gerda and maybe a new jazz album or two. He'd have to be careful.

Gerda made do with Russian stockings, but nothing could compare to the silks Degner had given her when he returned from Monza. She'd have preferred to have done her own shopping, but Berlin would never allow the two of them to travel out of the country together. Besides, who'd look after the boys? With both sets of grandparents gone, the only relatives she had left were now in the West.

Berlin assumed she'd never return. And they were right.

Gerda and Ernst did not talk about the possibility of defecting. That conversation took place in their most private thoughts without ever being voiced. Words like these were best left unsaid. Unspoken desires they could never explain were a kind of hope that would land them in jail. The Stasi had spies everywhere. They could hear East Germans breathe.

Gerda could tell, however, that Ernst's trips to the West were agitating him. He saw the money, the cars, and the clothes that the top riders were sporting. He was jealous. They had so much, and he had so little. He felt like a poor, country cousin and it rankled him to the core.

Gerda was grateful for the privileges that they enjoyed. The luxurious apartment, the *Wartburg* sedan, and even the media attention. Their fans adored them, and they were the darlings of the nation. It was an honour to be where they were, after all the hardships they had endured. She could hardly believe her good fortune and would not dream of asking for more.

For the most part, she was content with her home, her family, and her life. She was certain it could not get any better, or so she kept saying to herself. Although, at her most sentimental moments, she often thought it would be nice to see her aunts, uncles, and cousins again.

Degner, however, knew differently. As he scanned the shops in Douglas, he saw the goods ordinary citizens could buy. There were no queues lined up and down the street. There was more than enough produce on the shelves. People had choice when they shopped.

He couldn't believe his eyes when he entered the women's section of the clothing store, looking for pantyhose. The sizes, colours, brands, array, and varieties were dizzying. In Monza, he had Dita to help him. But here she was off gallivanting with that Jap-Whaddya-Call.

Deg was on his own. He picked up a couple pair, medium-priced and medium-sized, one dark colour, the other light. He didn't have a clue. He hoped they fit. Damn that Dita for not being here when he needed her.

Damn that Shepherd, too! Damn them all to Hell! That bunch of losers!

He paid and escaped the mystery of women's undergarments, hurrying out to the street.

He saw a record store and breathed a sigh of relief: ahhh, familiar territory. As he entered the shop, a bell on the door tinkled his arrival. Rows and rows of albums beckoned him. Chet Baker, John Coltrane, Miles Davis, Etta James. He had so many to choose from and so little money, he didn't know where to turn. He picked up *Sketches of Spain*. The album cover arrested him.

The yellow Spanish sky, the blood-soaked arena floor, the magnificent bull drawn inexorably towards the music, the trumpet an *espada* (sword).

The artist captured the thrilling anguish of the ritual that was about to occur, and it touched Degner's soul. The bull would be killed, and blood would flow. The carcass would be dragged out of the arena, and Miles Davis would bow and leave the audience to face its own blood-drenched mortality.

Alone.

— Do you like him, Matsumiya asked Degner, yanking him out of his trance.

— Bitte (pardon)?

— Miles Davis?

— Him? Ja, *natürlich* (Yes, naturally). Haven't heard this one yet.

— It's just been released. Would you like to? I'm Jimmy, by the way. Matsumiya.

He reached out his hand.

— Degner.

They shook hands.

— Ernst, I mean.

— I know who you are. I've seen you around the paddock. I met with Paul Petry. He thought you and I should talk. We're staying in the same hotel.

— Oh, you're with *Suzuki.*

Degner suddenly put face, name, and race together.

— What was your first clue?

Degner laughed uncomfortably. He'd never spoken to a Japanese person before.

— Would you like to listen to this album tonight? Over a drink in my room? I just bought a portable record player. He gestured to the case he was carrying. I'm eager to try it out before I return to England.

— *Ja,* sure. I better check with Herr Hartmann first.

— Your handler?

— *Der Sportkommissar der DDR* (East Germany's Sports commissioner). Otherwise, he'll be looking for me. I'll just pay for this and see you tonight.

— After dinner, then?

Degner headed to the till, pulling out his wallet. His hands were shaking. He breathed slowly, calmed his nerves, and handed over the cash. He could afford just one.

Matsumiya continued to look through the jazz section. When Degner left, he took *Sketches of Spain* to the till. When he left the store, he went up the street, not down.

22

Um Jeden Preis
(At Any Price)

Dita snuggled close to Degner's side while watching the Ultra Lightweight 125s race clockwise on the 37.73-mile long Snaefell Mountain course on the Isle of Man, the most dangerous motorcycle track in the world.

The only concession for safety is the odd straw bale or two at the worst corners. The margin for error while travelling at 88 feet or so per second is nil. Riders are out of luck if they overshoot their mark. There's no room to lay down their bikes on the verge and slide to a stop. They fly into stonewalls and shatter their arms, backs, hands, legs, necks, skulls, or wrists. While most rise to race again, many are too brain injured to think straight, and some die on the spot.

It's all in the unluck of the draw.

Flanked by two teammates, Carlo Ubbiali flew by on an *MV Agusta*. Two *MZ*s and five *Honda*s were hard on his tail.

Walter clicked his stopwatch.

— That's got to be 137 km/h, or so.

The official waved the checkered flag.

MZ's Hempleman drafted Taveri on an *MV Agusta* and proved to everyone in attendance that Walter Kaaden and his crew were a threat that could no longer be ignored.

What was his secret? Everyone wanted to know.

— That Kiwi, Hempleman sure can race, Petry said.

— .08 seconds separated him from the tenth-place competitor, Walter said.

— *MZ* could have easily come in third. We missed a podium finish by a hair.

— Less than that.

Just 0.2 of a second behind first place, Ray Fay blazed past in eighteenth place at 109 km/h on a *Colleda*.

— With a showing like that, Degner scoffed. They won't be winning a *World Championship* anytime soon. He ground his cigarette butt into the tarmac with the toe of his boot.

— I'm not so sure about that, Petry said. They have deep enough pockets to up their game any which way they choose.

He passed a flask to Degner, who took a swig and offered it to Walter, who refused. Petry had a sip and tucked it away.

— None for me? Dita asked. Not that I want any. Although, it would have been polite for you to offer.

— Too hot a burn for your spark, babe, Petry said. You need something with less fire.

Dita glowed.

— Can't argue with that.

Dressed like James Dean, Degner was the sexiest man in East Germany. Women adored him, men idolized him, and Dita had her work cut out for her.

When he wandered, it was up to Gerda, his wife and second love, to reel him back in. That was a combination that worked. If Gerda kept him from wandering too far from the paddock, so be it. They had *World Championships* to win.

Later, when Degner played the field solo, he was no good to anyone, least of all himself.

He was his own worst enemy.

But by then, Dita was on her way to fresh views and pastures new. Not one to be corralled and cornered, she yearned for a place of her own. One that had a view, where she could enjoy from a distance the rat race of this grand world.

— Whatever made them think that they could compete on the Isle of Man? Degner asked.

— It's what you do when you're in this business, Petry said. The *Tourist Trophy* is the motorcycle world's great proving ground.

— If you don't race here, you might as well stay home, Walter said. *Honda* entered the *TT* a few years back. In 1958, it was just as pitiful as *Suzuki* is today. Now look at them! They're improved. You start out losing, then you win one race after another, until someone else comes along and steals first from you. It's not called the Winner's Circle (of Life) for nothing.

— *Suzuki* will soon be lapping *Honda* right out of the picture, Petry said. Sure as shooting.

— The *TT* pushes all bikes to their limit, Dita said. But you aren't going anywhere if you don't have a seasoned rider. Racing on public roads through villages, carving through chicanes, and speed wobbling on straights are death-defying. This track is soaked in blood.

— Doesn't frighten me a bit, Degner said. When my number's up, it's all over. Until then, I'll race like there's no tomorrow.

He sneered as the last of the *Colledas* limped across the line.

— They aren't exactly in last place.

— Despite their poor showing, they are not doing badly.

— What I'd like to know is how we ended up in the same hotel? Degner asked. The organizers must have done it on purpose. Wouldn't put it past them. Us Krauts with them Japs.

— Want to camp out in the paddock again? Walter asked. The Fernleigh isn't exactly what you call second-rate.

— Except *MV Agusta* and *Norton* are in Douglas. And we're stuck out here in the middle of nowhere.

— Maybe that's all that was left when we got around to registering, Dita said. The big names booked their rooms last year. Bet they have standing reservations.

She leaned into Degner, but he pushed back, irritated.

— We're bunking with the newcomers, Walter said. That's all. We have no reason for complaint. Just remember what we're here for. In and of itself, simply entering the *TT* is huge.

— And Hartmann? Degner asked.

— As *Sportkommissar*, he has the long view. He knows we won't win this skirmish, but we better do well in the overall battle. If we don't show, heads will roll.

— His, too?

— Losing is the unpardonable sin. The *Rennkollektiv* has one purpose. Berlin wants podium finishes and victorious East Germans in the headlines.

— It's all sports and politics? Isn't it? Dita asked.

— You'd be naive not to think so, Petry said. Berlin can't compete in the theatre of war, but it can in the sports arena. It's all marketing. Life in East Germany under Communism is better than anything the West could ever offer.

— We may have one of the smallest populations in Europe, but we're the powder keg. What happens at home, for good or ill, has international repercussions.

— The Russians and Americans are at each other's throats. Germans on both sides are caught in the middle. Not to mention the rest of the world.

— There's no such thing as a level playing field. Each side plays dirty. Winning is all.

— So, what you're saying is that no matter how competitive *MZ* becomes, we'll eventually lose? Degner asked.

— There's always an up-and-comer ready to take on the leader.

What's the use of staying on a sinking ship? Degner thought as he shifted from one foot to another. Dita pushed hard into him. He set her up on her centre stand and stepped away.

— You need to keep your wits about you, no matter what, she whispered.

— All I know is that Hartmann's head will never be on the chopping block.

— He's probably got a Swiss bank account for when he needs to escape.

— If that's so, why doesn't he defect?

— He's making more money in East Germany than he ever could in the West.

— He prefers life in the shadows, Dita said. Out of sight, out of mind. Yet close to those in power. In the West, he's a nobody. Out in the dark without a friend. And no way to line his pockets. Staying in East Berlin is to his benefit. He's close to the money.

Degner looked at his watch.

— Anybody else hungry? I'm starving.

— It's been a long time since I tucked into that Manx breakfast, Petry admitted.

— I heard someone say it's better than the English one, Dita said.

— How would you know? Degner asked. You're not exactly a gourmand.

— You're right. Too much octane gives me gas. However, I'd try a banger off your plate any day of the week, no matter how small it is.

She sifted a ripe one that caught Degner off guard. He stepped back and pulled a wrench out of his pocket. You maybe need a thicker gasket before your next race.

— As long as you don't over-torque me, *kleines Liebchen* (little darling). I'll go the distance with you anytime, anywhere. Just say the word.

— Full Manx or Full English, the French will eat neither, Petry said. Can't imagine what they say about a Scots breakfast. They think German cuisine is a weapon of mass destruction.

— They haven't had my Inge's *Schnitzel,* Walter boasted. Her *Rotkohl* (red cabbage) is unbelievable. And her *Rouladen* with hot buttered *Spätzle? Ach du lieber Gott* (Oh my dear God)!

— The Swedes came up with the smorgasbord. Though their *Prinskorv* (Prince Sausage) might be too small for you, Dita.

— There's quantity, then there's quality.

— I want it all, Degner said. The shops at home leave a lot to be desired.

— Then you better stay away from the Japanese, Dita said. Their food is art. It satisfies the eye but not the stomach. It tantalizes but keeps you hungering for more.

Walter shifted Dita off her stand.

— With all this talk about food, I'm getting hungry.

He rolled her to the paddock, where the other team members were congratulating Hempleman on his near win. They were as excited as schoolboys perusing Susan Kelly's centrefold.

Only Degner was out of sorts.

Dita knew better than to try and cheer him up. Some men like to sulk, especially when they feel short-changed.

MZ's immediate challenge was to keep *Suzuki* from beating them at their own game. While Walter may not have been the father of the two-stroke engine, he knew them better than anyone else on the planet. His secrets were ripe for the plucking.

— Did you see Herr Suzuki riding with the cameraman? Degner asked. With that piece of flash? What's his name? Matsamoto?

— Matsumiya! Dita corrected him.

— Yeah. I keep forgetting.

— Fancy dresser, fast talker, Petry said. And the thickest wad of British pounds, I have ever seen.

— With that kind of money, *Suzuki* can afford to take on *Honda.*

— But *Honda*'s unassailable, Dita said. Mike the Bike Hailwood and Jim Redman win nearly every race they enter. I hear that *Honda* looks after its racers, even those injured on the track. They have a future when their racing careers are over.

— Saw that Matsumiya character at a record shop today. Looking at albums. He's invited me up to his room this evening for a listen. That new Davis album. He's bought the latest record player. The sound is supposed to be incredible.

— Make sure you clear it with Hartmann first, Walter said. I don't want any misunderstandings that could send us packing.

— Hartmann and me? We're tight. Besides *Suzuki* has nothing to offer. They're a catastrophe waiting to happen.

— But they have money, money, money, whispered Dita in his ear. He brushed her off.

— Give them time, Walter said. They'll soon be showing us a thing or two.

Petry took a quick swig from his flask before passing it to Degner.

— What frightens me, Petry said. Those aluminum skins with wings flying thousands of metres above an empty ocean.

— Good thing the Continental Circus is in Europe, Walter said. So far, the only things we've had to worry about are mountain passes, border controls, and ferries.

— But if the *GP* goes trans-Atlantic?

— Maybe aviation will get safer. It's gotta, just like motorcycle racing.

— Say whatever you want about *Suzuki,* Degner said. That Matsumiya has good taste in music.

— But Miles Davis? Petry asked. Chet Baker, maybe. Not that Davis!

— Are you sure it wasn't any Petula Clark he was after?

Degner laughed.

— She's too much like Shirley Temple for my taste.

— She's no longer a child, Petry said. Have you ever listened to her "*Seemann Deine Heimat*"?

— (Sailor, Your Home)? Dita caterwauled.

Degner put his hands over his ears and begged her to stop.

— Oh, Dita, please! He wept. Motorcycling may have ruined my hearing, but I still have ears to hear.

— If you want hot, chase after her now, Dita said. Me and Alfred were fooling around in Heidelberg. She was on a set. Completely naked in skin-tight leathers. She'd take a boy anywhere he dreams.

— Middle-aged men, too? Petry said.

— You lot aren't above making fools of yourselves. Better stay close to Fidele, though. You won't find anyone better. You too, Deg. Don't go messing around. Gerda's the best thing that ever happened to you. Uncle Walter! Just listen to me.

Except they couldn't.

They left women spellbound and gasping whenever they entered a room.

Or so they thought.

23

Paseíllo

(The Opening Procession)

That evening, Degner followed Matsumiya out of the dining room.

Hartmann had given his young charge the nod. He and that Japanese fellow could listen to whatever god-awful jazz album they wanted. Just show up for work in the morning. That's all he asked.

— What I've learned, he said, as he filled Dita's glass with *White Lightening,* is to cut my stars some slack. If you constantly refuse them, they'll eventually snap. All Hell will break loose. This way, I've reduced the pressure. By letting them blow off some steam, I've averted a problem before it's arisen and they're happy.

— *Herzlichen Glückwunsch* (Congratulations), Herr Hartmann! *Du bist ein geborener Anführer* (You are a natural-born leader).

— Deg's too hungry for this year's *World Championship* to jeopardize his chances. With the points he's already accumulated, he could be wearing the laurel wreath at the season's end.

Dita raised her glass to him.

Hartmann raised his to her.

— To Degner, she said.

— To winning, he replied.

He drained his glass in one gulp and she touched hers to her lips. Eeew, another drink with too much fire power. She tried again.

— A gal could go blind drinking this.

And pushed it away.

Hartmann poured himself another and settled back into his chair.

Matsumiya and Degner climbed the stairs together, two at a time. Just before the top, Degner sprinted ahead.

— Aha! He yelled. *Wie gewöhnlich* (As usual)! *Ich bin an erster Stelle* (I'm in first place).

They continued down the hallway.

— Here we are, Matsumiya said. He pulled out the key to his room, opened the door, and invited Degner to enter.

— Sit there. He pointed to the sofa. Relax while I set this up. Would you like an *Okell's?* It's a Manx beer. I stopped by the brewery earlier today.

— Certainly, Degner smacked his lips. I can hardly wait.

Matsumiya opened a bottle and grabbed a glass, but Degner stopped him.

74

— Don't bother. I'll drink this one straight up. You can pour my second one.

Matsumiya smiled and focussed on his new *Crosley Stack-O-Matic* portable record player.

— Seen this before?

Degner shook his head and leaned in for a closer look.

— No, I haven't. Does it really hold six records at a time?

— That's what the specs say. It has a belt-driven turntable and a fully automatic tonearm.

— Really? I wonder how's the sound with that single speaker.

— Surprisingly good. But if we had a pair of *Bang & Olufsens*, we'd be in heaven.

— You're telling me. Mono's on the way out. Stereo's where it's at.

— This *Crosley* may be portable, but it has a full dynamic range with an adjustable tone control. The sound is amazing.

— *Du klingst genau wie der Verkäufer* (You sound just like the salesman), *den ich neulich getroffen habe* (that I met the other day).

— What can I say? It's what I do for a living. Every day, I tell a story to sell something. Convincing others they can't live without what I'm offering.

— Like that diamond-stylus needle? For just a few pennies more? A deal too good to pass up?

— It makes all the difference when you want to hear the sound as it was recorded. Matsumiya rotated the *On / Off Volume* knob clockwise. It clicked and the record player hummed. He lifted the tension arm and rotated it counter clockwise back over the tonearm.

— Pass me the record.

— Oh, *ja*. Degner stopped reading the liner notes and handed it to Matsumiya. He took the LP out of the cover and removed the thin onion paper sleeve. He was careful to handle the record by its edges, not getting his fingers on the tracks.

— Mustn't compromise the sound quality. Nothing compares to listening to a record the first time it's played.

— Although some things get better the more you do them. First times can often be such disappointments. Like lovemaking. You've got to get the first one out of the way before you can move on to the good stuff.

— Not with these long new long play records, Matsumiya said.

He loaded the album onto the central spindle and rotated the tension arm back over the record, where it dropped automatically into place. He turned the *Select Size* switch to twelve, the *Speed* to thirty-three rpm, and the *Turntable* switch to On. After he removed the protective needle cover, he twisted the *Turntable* switch to Automatic.

— I haven't quite figured out how to do this manually, he confessed.

— It takes a steady hand. You need a dust brush though. We don't want any unnecessary surface noise.

— You're telling me. I have one, but not here. It's back home.

— There shouldn't be any lint on this record. It's brand new. Besides, you can just blow it off. That's how we do it.

— You have a record player?

— A *Kuba Comet* I bought in West Germany. Cost a fortune. Not a portable like this. Had the boys heave it into our transport truck. They carried it up the stairs into our apartment. Drank beer and listened to some Heino. Gerda loves his *Schlager* (Hits).

The tonearm lifted; the record dropped to the turntable, and the stylus moved over to the first song. Once it set down, the bright and unsettling first notes from Miles Davis' trumpet filled the room.

Matsumiya turned the volume up higher. He grabbed two more beers and poured them into glasses. Handed one to Degner.

Degner sipped this one as they listened to *Concierto de Aranjuez.*

— How mournful, Matsumiya said.

— I'm the matador, ready for the *estocada* (the fatal lunge of the sword in a bullfight).

Matsumiya nodded. They lit their cigarettes.

The music turned ominous, percussive, and discordant. A feeling of grief and impending doom filled the smoke-filled room. Matsumiya turned the volume even louder.

— Petry says you want out.

— I want to ride motorcycles that win and make more money than I can spend.

— *Suzuki* has the resources to give you the world.

— On those *Colledas?*

— No. On machines that you would design.

— That I would design? Now that's a fascinating idea. What's in it for me?

— Ten thousand British pounds?

— I'm interested. What else?

— What do you want?

— A riding contract for next year.

— That's a lot of money. Do you know what you're asking?

— I do, but I'm risking my family. They need to get out of East Germany.

— Mr. Suzuki will only agree to this if you deliver something significant and on time.

— Will Kaaden's latest specs do?

— For starters. How about some new pistons? To analyze their metallurgy.

— No problem.

— And you design a 125cc 22 hp engine?

— I'm already working on one.

— You and Petry can build ours this winter.

— At your factory? In Japan?

— Naturally.

— That means we'd have to fly?

— An ocean liner would take too long.

— With your facilities, I can build whatever you want.

— Don't promise anything you can't deliver.

— A 125cc twenty-two horsepower and unlimited access to *Suzuki*'s resources and technicians? I can do that.

— Then we have a deal?

— We have a deal.

They shook hands.

— I'll draw up a contract, get Mr. Suzuki's approval, and see you in Assen.

— I'll talk to Gerda about getting her and the boys out of the country. They'll board the train in East Berlin and mingle with the crowds commuting to their jobs in the West.

— Just don't break your arm when you're in Assen. We need your signature on the contract.

— Assen, first on June 24, then Spa-Francorchamps on July 2.

— Can you get everything together by then?

— How about 13 August? Just to be sure. That'd give me an extra month to copy the plans without raising suspicions and get Gerda and the boys out of the country.

— Well, the sooner, the better. During the *GP* at Dundrod, then. We need you in Japan, to build that engine.

— But not before the *World Championship*, Degner insisted. I'm neck-and-neck with Tom Phillis. Taveri and Redman aren't far behind. Hailwood, Shepherd, and Brehme are also threats. I need all the points I can get.

— I can see that you've done your arithmetic.

— I'm this close, Herr Matsumiya, this close. I can't afford to miss any races this season.

— Sign the contract in Assen and defect when you're in Ireland. We can make it happen.

— 13 August 1961, it is. Then I start riding for *Suzuki*.

— I'll be waiting for Gerda and the boys at the station in West Berlin and will have a dozen long-stemmed roses to give her. That's my promise.

— No, Degner said. Have Petry meet her. She trusts him.

— And not me?

Degner didn't answer.

The music stopped.

— I better get back.

— Oh, wait a sec. Take this.

Matsumiya handed Degner the album.

Degner brushed against Matsumiya as he charged out the door.

24

Die Freiheit ist nur eine Zugfahrt entfernt
(Freedom is just a Train Ride Away)

— Are you sure you can get everything ready for 13 August? Gerda asked.

— Of course, Degner said. This isn't magic. I've been watching Kaaden for years.

— He's taught you everything you know.

— That's true. And I'm a helluva student. As Kaaden always says, *Je besser Sie die mechanischen Prozesse verstehen* (The more you understand the mechanical processes), *desto besser werden Sie* (the better you'll become).

— What if something unforeseen happens? You don't have any margin for error.

— Have I ever? In my line of work, you're right on or dead. It's the in-between that's my worst nightmare. Surviving but never fully recovering. Alive but not being able to race.

— You need a contingency plan. That's how we survived the war. We always had an escape route in mind.

— I'll spend every minute I'm not on the track in the shop finishing my racer. It's already got 25 hp, but the Japanese don't need to know that. Kaaden won't suspect a thing with me scouring the specs. He'll think it's for my bike. In fact, I'll get him to coach me on the finer points. That'll hook him.

— And while you're working, I'll watch out for you.

— Maybe I'll even learn how to back off on the throttle.

— You think? Gerda smiled.

— *Der alte Mann* (the old man) will walk me through the process, one step at a time. Before he suspects a thing, I'll know the plans inside out. I'll pocket a couple pistons from the scrap heap. They won't be missed.

— Just make sure they're the right ones.

— For God's sake, Degner bristled at the rasping sound of her voice. Of course, dear.

— But can you build the engine that *Suzuki* wants? This winter? Are you prepared to spend the off-season alone in Japan?

— Gerda, we've been through this a thousand times before. I'll do what needs to be done.

79

— But what about the boys and me while you're away? We'll be all alone.

— Alone? You have your family in the West.

— They're busy with their own lives. They won't have time for us.

— Once they know you're around, they'll make a place for you. We'll find an apartment near them. They'll give you a job. Before you know it, you'll have your feet planted on the ground.

— And then what? You're not going to abandon me, are you? Once you have found fame and fortune? Are you, Deg?

— Never Gerda. I couldn't leave you or the boys. Not for all the tea ...

— In Japan? That's small comfort, Ernst. Your words are fine, but sometimes you frighten me. You're uncontrollable. I realize there's no future for us here. As much as I love Walter, we must get out before it's too late. But what about him and Inge?

— He'll find his own way. He always has. There's the *International Six Days Trials* if *Grand Prix* road-racing goes sideways. He can make his name in that sport. It's still motorcycling.

— You mean we're not indispensable for his continued well-being?

— Not at all. He's too smart to place his destiny in the hands of a single person.

— Then we better take a lesson out of his playbook.

— What do you mean?

— Paul Petry. I know him. He won't always be there for you.

— Pardon?

— He has his limits. You can't push him. He has only so much to give.

— He's been very good to us so far.

— All I know is that he won't be travelling to Japan with you.

— What do you mean? I don't get that.

— When we were out having drinks with him? I listened to what he had to say. Do you even know the name of his wife?

— He's married?

— Her name is Fidele, Ernst. She's a good sensible woman.

— Really, I would never have guessed.

— He's still shaken after those plane crashes. Manchester United, Ritchie Valens, and Buddy Holly, they're all dead. I tell you, he's afraid of flying.

— He's got that right. Airplanes are unsafe at any altitude. I'd rather fly low on a bike.

— The point is. You need to listen to others. You aren't the only person in the room.

— Guess that means I'll be eating raw fish alone in Hamamatsu.

— And in the meantime? I better get the boys on the train to West Berlin.

— When you're in the station, just don't panic. You'll be among thousands commuting to the west. Breathe in through the nose and exhale through the mouth. I tell you it works every time. Slows the heart rate. Once you've crossed the line, you're free.

— I like the sound of that. Freedom.

— It's just a train ride away.

25

Ihre Besten Interessen
(Your Best Interests)

— Deg, you wretch! Dita screeched as her engine seized. Metal against metal, scraping at 11,000 rpm. Why didn't you listen?

Before Degner could pull in the clutch, he flew headlong over her handlebars and pounded into the pavement. The radius in his right arm snapped when he landed. Dita scraped to a stop.

When she came to, she felt Walter dragging her off the track.

— Let's get you out of here before something worse happens.

The marshals pulled Degner to safety and ambulance sirens were sounding.

Tom Phillis and Jim Redman blazed past on *Honda*s. Alan Shepherd and Werner Musiol flew on *MZ*s. Phil Read rocketed by on an *EMC*, a *DKW*-knock off.

Joe Ehrlich MZ's archnemesis re-engineered *DKW's Rennsporte Ladempumpe* bikes. He raced them with the *Ehrlich Motorcycle Co* logo on their tanks.

— Leave me alone, *Onkel*. Don't let Deg out of your sight. That Matsumiya.... She passed out before she could finish.

Matsumiya watched the events unfold from the sidelines. As soon the ambulance pulled up to where Degner was lying prone on the track, he grabbed the folder full of papers beside him and ran to his car. He headed straight to the hospital, arriving there just as the ambulance attendants rushed Degner into the Emergency.

Matsumiya bided his time. As soon as there was a lull in the action, he slipped unnoticed to Degner's left side.

— Deg, are you awake?

Degner nodded.

— Can you hold a pen?

— They've given me a shot of morphine and told me to rest.

— Just sign this. Quickly. Before they return. You need to trust me. I've got your best interests in mind.

Degner scrawled his signature on the piece of paper. It was nearly illegible. But his contract with *Suzuki* was now binding and in full effect.

They shook hands and Matsumiya stuffed the contract into his jacket pocket.

He was about to leave when Walter pulled back the curtains around Degner's bed.

— What the Hell Matsumiya! What are you doing here?

— Checking on the patient, Herr Kaaden. Matsumiya rose from the chair, bowed, and slipped out.

— Deg? What's going on? Dita said something about you and Matsumiya.

Degner didn't answer. The morphine stole him away before he could incriminate himself.

26

Geschichtsmacher
(History Maker)

— Oh, there you are! Petry said in a loud voice as he strode through the *MZ* workshop. Using his good hand, Degner inserted the last of the bolts into Dita's cylinder head.

— Almost done? She asked. After that fiasco in Assen, I'd like to get back on the track.

— I was in to see Herr Kaaden. I need more *MZ*s. Because of you, Deg, I can't get enough. They sell as soon as I put them on the floor. Thought I'd drop by to see how you're doing. Kaaden said you've been working in the shop since you were released.

— Gotta wear this cast for a few more weeks. Now that Dita's repaired, I can finish my racer. She'll soon run like someone stole her. Then I'll take it apart. Care to bring it in pieces to Saarbrucken? I'll sell it in the West for some hard currency. I could use some extra cash.

— What for? Dita asked, perking up.

Degner didn't answer.

— Yeah, sure. If I'm searched, I'll say it's parts for my shop. I service the bikes I sell.

Dita became concerned. She could sense that Degner was no longer thinking about the task at hand. His mind was wandering.

— Check that torque wrench, numb-nuts. I'd hate to have you strip anymore threads out of my engine block.

— Man, you're a hard motorcycle to please. A fellow makes one mistake, and you never let him forget it.

— Sounds like Fidele. I made her walk home after our second anniversary dinner. Had to see a guy about a bike. Couldn't pass up the deal, you know, and she still hasn't forgiven me.

— That's harsh, Degner said. Did you get the bike?

Petry looked over his shoulder before nodding.

— Good mechanicking, Deg, that's all I'm asking, Dita said. But don't force me. When was the last time that you had that thing calibrated? No more than *twenty newton meters*, if you know what's good for you.

— Would you be happy with *two kilo-pond meters*? That's the wrench I have.

— Are you trying to be funny? They're one and the same but stripping threads in soft aluminum is no joke. You need to focus. She fumed in silence while Degner tightened her head.

— You two sound like an old bickering couple. He grabbed the wrench from Degner. Let me give it a go. I know a thing or two about tuning engines.

— Just make sure you're up to speed when we go on our little trip, Degner whispered.

— Ya? About that? I'm actually having second thoughts. Maybe there's another...

Degner grabbed Petry by the arm and dragged him outside, away from Dita's cocked ears.

— What do you mean? Degner looked Petry straight in the eyes.

— Flying thousands of kilometres over an empty ocean doesn't exactly fill me with confidence.

— You're saying this now when everything's planned? You can't back out. Cut that crap right away.

— I'm not sure I can pull it all off. Everything else? Sure. But Japan? I don't know.

— Now you listen. You're in this. You can't stop. Don't screw around with me. You got that?

— Yeah, Deg, yeah. I was just talking. You think the train station's the way to go? It's a Sunday, the thirteenth, not exactly an auspicious number.

— The *Ostbahnhof* (East Train Station) is busy seven days a week. Even the worst job in West Berlin is better than anything here. They pay in Deutschmarks, not Ostmarks. It's a good deal for everyone. The West gets cheap labour, and the East gets a currency worth something. The money's irresistible.

Degner fumbled for his cigarettes.

— Can't stay out here for long. Dita will get suspicious.

They walked back into the shop. Degner saw the smokes on the work bench where he had left them. He offered one to Petry.

— Okay, I get it, Petry assured Degner. You will beat Phillis in the 125. That's a given.

— At least Walter doesn't have me racing against Shepherd.

— He's protecting your points, Deg. The team's behind you. You're his best chance. Don't you see? Alan's racing in the 350 against Mike Duff. They're both riding for *AJS*.

— The guy with the yellow leaf on his helmet? The Canadian?

— Have you seen him ride? He's a history-maker, that one.

— You have no idea, Dita said. The distress he feels. He'd do anything to find happiness. Ride the world's fastest motorcycle. Born a boy was the worst thing that happened to him.

— Huh? Both Degner and Petry looked at her.

— He'd ride for *Norton* in the morning and *MV Agusta* in the afternoon, if it meant he'd get a win. He's not one to let old loyalties get in the way.

— That Shepherd doesn't have a chance, Petry snorted.

Degner smiled.

— Not a hope in Hell.

Petry pulled Degner aside.

— Ever seen one of these? It's a miniature *Crystar.* Matsumiya asked me to give it to you. This way you won't have to steal Kaaden's actual plans. Just take pictures.

27

Beiwagen
(Sidecar)

— Want to try something new? Degner asked Gerda. I had one while I was on the Isle of Man.

— Certainly, *Liebling*. She crossed her legs. What do you have for me this time?

Degner combined cognac, *Triple Sec*, and freshly squeezed lemon juice in a cocktail shaker. He added some ice and shook it. Then strained it into two cut crystal glasses before handing her one.

She took a sip.

— *Lecker* (Delicious)! What is it?

— A Sidecar, a *TT* cocktail.

They both laughed.

— Should I have chilled the glasses, though?

— I'm cold enough. She snuggled up to him on the couch. How about that new album?

He turned the *Kuba Comet* on and the tubes warmed up.

— You'll like this one.

He took the LP out of its inner sleeve and handed her the cover. She smiled as he placed the record on the turntable, dusted it off with his state-of-the-art carbon fibre lint brush, and set the tonearm down on the second track. They listened to Davis's upbeat yet melancholic "Will o' the Wisp" and sipped their drinks. He turned the volume up.

— Gerda, honestly, he whispered. Do you think you can pull this off?

— I'm married to a motorcycle racer. I look death straight in the face every time you bump start your bike. Of course, I can. The question is, can you?

— There's no other way for you to get out. All the borders have been sealed except those from East into West Berlin. You'll have to join the other East Berliners commuting to their jobs. Just blend in with the crowd and no one will notice.

— Don't you even think about delaying the defection for a few extra points. You want to win the *World Championship*, of course. But for once, think of your family.

— We're in this together. You do your part. I'll do mine. And soon, our boys will be free.

— Will Paul be waiting?

87

— With a dozen roses. You won't miss him.

— Good. The 13th of August 1961 is an auspicious date for us to start our new life. On the twelfth, the boys and I will check into the *Hotel zur Ostbahn.*

— Even though you're travelling on a Sunday, there'll be lots of people at the station. Remember! Pack for a day trip.

— And Dita? Does she know?

— No question she suspects something's up. You can't slip anything past her.

— Gerda took a long sip of her drink. The citrusy flavour made her pucker her lips. Perhaps a little more sugar?

Degner kissed her hot on the mouth.

She pulled him to her, and they continued on to have the ride of their lives, at first slow and leisurely. And then, a head long rush to a dramatic conclusion. The way of life in the fast lane.

28

Blauer Himmel und Sonnenschein
(Blue Skies and Sunshine)

— One second behind Takahashi on that *Honda*, Dita said. We could have overtaken him, but we ran out of track.

— 1.2 seconds, Degner replied, correcting her.

— But three ahead of Phillis and Redman.

She laughed.

— You'd think Hailwood never raced at Dundrod before.

— 48.4 seconds, Deg. You were amazing.

— And Taveri? We beat him by a minute twenty-two.

— We were so far ahead he couldn't see my rear end. How disappointing for that poor boy.

— Takahashi just had a lucky break. That's all.

— He's no real contender in the points classification. We thrashed the riders that counted.

— I'm on my way to the *World Championship*. It's so close I can taste it.

— Makes you wonder, though, doesn't it? You and your Sunday scheming.

— What do you mean?

— With *Suzuki*, you don't have a chance.

— Didn't think I had one with *MZ* either. Who'd have thought last spring we'd be this close? Had I known, I'd have held Matsumiya off.

— Once Gerda and the boys get on the train tomorrow, there's no turning back. Just don't do anything rash. Don't go second-guessing yourself.

— I can't phone her from Ireland. That's out of the question. It'd draw too much attention. Raise suspicions. And put them in more danger than they already are. If anything should happen, I'd never forgive myself. If I sent a telegram to the hotel? Hint about a delay? I'm so close to winning.

— And alert the authorities that something's up? In case you've forgotten, she's under surveillance. The Stasi have eyes on her. Hartmann told me in not so many words.

— They won't suspect a thing, Dita.

— You can't be sure, Deg. You better assume that they are watching her every move.

— What a nightmare. I can't defect when I'm this close to winning.

— Do you want to jeopardize the safety of your family?

— She'd survive without me, you know. She has family in the West. They'd set her up.

— Don't be a fool, Degner. You can't abandon her. You started this. Now finish it.

— This close, Dita, this close. *MZ* can't survive without me. I'll play the innocent and say that Gerda defected without me knowing.

— What'll you tell Matsumiya?

— That the Stasi closed ranks around me once they heard Gerda and the boys escaped.

— You'll never race internationally again.

— I wouldn't be so sure about that. Kaaden and Hartmann love all that I've done for them. I'm their darling.

— But what about Moscow? It'll take those guys down with you. Berlin couldn't care less about motorcycle racing. They're looking for any reason to cancel this program. Don't give them one.

Degner lit a cigarette and handed it to Dita. She drew back on the smoke. It calmed her down.

Then it hit her. She looked at Degner. She finally had this boy all to herself.

She wanted to eat him up and have his taste linger in her mouth.

But Gerda and the boys? She wasn't her sister's keeper.

Sometimes in the heat of the moment even motorcycles go cockeyed. Things fall apart.

At this very instant, Gerda's absence was Dita's unlucky break. With proximity as the catalyst for desire, she stubbed her cigarette out.

The very thing she knew she shouldn't be doing.

— Oh, what the Hell!

Once she started, he couldn't stop. Off came his clothes, from his head to his feet. In a mad rush, she inhaled Degner to the end of the line.

He begged for more and she savoured the electricity of his caress.

They closed their eyes and tried to block the outside world from crashing in. The guilt and the betrayal made the thrill even more pleasurable.

Then they drifted off to sleep.

Then the door to the hotel room yawned open.

Then Matsumiya stepped inside.

— Hey, Dita! Deg! You here?

A voice tinged with an Oxford accent roused them awake.

— Jimmy? Degner asked. What are you doing here?

— Just checking. The door was unlocked.

Degner stumbled to the bathroom, pulling on his clothes. He rinsed the metallic tang out of his mouth. So bitter and yet so sweet. He splashed some cold water on his face and ran a comb through his hair. Refreshed, he walked out to greet Matsumiya.

— You okay?

— Just Dita and me. We're hanging out.

Matsumiya couldn't care less about what they were doing behind closed curtains. As long as Degner kept his part of the bargain, he could dally with anything he wanted.

— Shepherd and that Mike Duff battled it out on a pair of 350s. What a race! Duff's the best *GP* racer to come out of Toronto.

— I'm surprised Walter didn't get him riding with *MZ*. He's that good.

— I wouldn't say no to a person like that, Dita said, smoothing out her fairing. If he is anything like the two Canadians I knew during the war, he can give me all the language lessons he wants.

— I'll introduce you if you like. On the ferry back to England tomorrow?

— It'll be a great coming out morning, Dita said. All sunshine and blue sky. Maybe even a rainbow.

29

Operation Rose

The hotel alarm clock roused Gerda. All night long, she'd been drifting in and out of sleep. Startled, she fumbled to turn the alarm off. She needed a few minutes to clear her head before she awoke the boys. She saw Olaf and Boris sleeping soundly. Then she heard the old, all-too-familiar roar of *Soviet T-54s,* the sound of their continuous tracks, steel clattering on cobblestones. The haze of diesel exhaust fouling the air.

— Oh no, she groaned. Not today. Please God, not today. Of all days.

She ran to the window, pulled back the curtains, and looked down to the street below. Soldiers were patrolling while heavy military vehicles thundered past. Gerda turned the radio on and listened to the broadcast.

— The inner-city border between East and West Berlin is now sealed. Trains are no longer running between the two sectors.

She stumbled to the toilet and threw up.

Olaf woke to hear his mother heaving her guts out and sobbing. He tugged her back to bed and under the covers. Hugging and comforting her, he loved her as only a child could. Without compromise.

— *Komm Mama, bitte* (Come on Mum, please), *was ist los* (what's going on)?

Boris slept through the commotion.

The broken-hearted mother and her stalwart two-year-old son wailed in the dawning light of the brilliant red sun as it rose in the eastern sky.

30

Vollgas Voraus
(Full Speed Ahead)

— It was just bad luck, Degner said to Gerda while she fed Boris.

Their older son Olaf raced the Sachsenring in the grass at their feet. They were sitting on a bench in the park outside their apartment building.

— I don't know if I can do this again, Gerda replied. Waking up to those tanks brought everything all back. The fear and the dread. I'd rather just disappear. She shuddered at the thought.

— The easy way is no longer an option. The border around West Berlin is sealed. We cannot turn back.

— Barbed wire, machine guns, and Alsatians. We're prisoners in our own country.

Degner glanced at his watch.

— Look, dear, I must go. Kaaden's expecting me. Will you be okay?

— Fine! Just give me that smoke of yours.

Degner handed her his cigarette and hugged her. He kissed Boris and tousled Olaf's blonde hair.

— *Pass auf deine Mutter und deinen Bruder auf* (Look after your mother and brother).

Olaf smiled.

— *Ja, Papa* (Yes, Daddy)!

Degner sprinted to their *Wartburg* sedan that was parked on the road. Gerda pulled a flask out of her purse and poured a long, delicious torrent down her throat. She leaned back, slowly tightened the cap back on and relaxed, luxuriating in the warm, late summer sun.

There won't be many more days like this, she mused.

— *Papa!* Olaf yelled as he scrambled to his feet and ran as fast as he could after his father.

— *Du hast das vergessen* (You forgot this)!

He held out a cast metal motorcycle in his outstretched hand, racing into the street and stopping dead in the traffic.

Degner's attention was already focused on his work at the shop. How would he build a twenty-two horsepower 125cc engine in Japan without Paul Petry? The stress and the worry wore him down. And now, with the border sealed off and patrolled by soldiers with machine guns, it was all too much for him to bear. His family was at risk, and he didn't know where to turn. He gambled their safety for a pipe dream. Now it turned into a compression chamber, and he was about to lose everything that really mattered.

Horns blared. Tires screeched. Olaf stood there, devastated, his blue eyes full of tears, watching his father accelerate around the bend and disappear down the road. Vehicles of all sizes and shapes fouled the air with their black exhaust and careened down upon the little blonde boy dressed in *lederhosen*, holding a small toy in his hand.

Gerda, suddenly alert and completely sober, chased after Olaf. With Boris under one arm, she grabbed Olaf by the collar with the other. She yanked him out of the path of an approaching truck without a moment to spare. It thundered past at full speed, the driver ashen faced.

31

Großes Schwarzes Auto
(Big Black Car)

Gerda twisted the cap off a bottle of vodka. She was about to tip it down her throat when Degner grabbed for it.

The radio was blaring.

— For God's sake, Gerda, what are you thinking?

— Give that back.

— Get a grip on yourself, woman. You can't do this drunk. You need to sober up. Think of the children. They need you. I need you.

— Leave me be, her words slurred together. She made a swipe for the bottle, but Degner pulled it away from her.

— *Du bist nicht der Einzige* (You aren't the one), *der stundenlang in diese Sardinenbüchse gestopft wird* (who'll be stuffed in that sardine can for hours on end).

— It's one hundred kilometres from Berlin on the transit corridor to the border. One hour, Gerda. That's why Petry chose it. The shortest route available. Once you enter the corridor from East Berlin, it's clear sailing to Helmstedt-Marienborn, the largest border crossing between East and West Germany.

— And if the boys start to cry?

— We'll slip them a Mickey Finn. They'll sleep the whole way.

— But will they wake up? How do we know it's the right dose? And the border control? What about them and their dogs? Have you thought about that?

— They'll be fine. Petry knows what he's doing.

— *Was ist Plan B*, Ernst? When I'm shipped off to Siberia, our boys will be God knows where. And you'll be in the West with that bitch Dita. Don't you think I don't know what you two have been up to?

Degner tried to calm her down. She refused.

— Petry's already driving regularly through the checkpoint with his car.

— On his way to the *Leipziger Messe* (Leipzig Trade Fair)? She asked, her head clearing.

He nodded.

— He's a familiar sight. That new Lincoln with the big block V-8 he bought from some soldier stationed at Ramstein is such a spectacle. It's all that the guards notice. Chrome and white-walled tires and leather seats. It's huge.

— They won't find the hidden compartment in the trunk?

— Those guards will be so tied up with the front end they won't remember it has a back. The car causes such a sensation they won't notice the false floor even if they did open the lid.

— How'll he divert their attention?

— You know Petry. He takes centre stage. He knows how to tell a story and bring it to a profitable conclusion. And he likes to talk. Everyone sees him. That's all they ever notice. Then he sells himself. People get to know him. He makes a good first impression.

— You're telling me. He wears a fine suit. I liked him as soon as I laid my eyes upon him.

— Within five minutes he's on a first-name basis with everyone he meets.

— Even Germans?

— Especially Germans, Degner laughed. It's no wonder he's so successful. By the time I get to Monza, he'll be such a familiar sight that the guards will buy anything he offers to sell them. You don't have a thing to worry about.

— And Dita? What about her?

— What about her?

— Are you going to abandon me for that battered piece of sheet metal?

— She's just a motorcycle, for God's sake, Gerda. I ride her to win but not to love.

— But when have I ever had you for my own?

— You've known this all along. You shouldn't be surprised. I can do no other. Winning is everything.

— I'm not surprised. Dita's been good to you. I hate and adore her. She's stolen your heart. That's all you think about, being one with her and riding her all the way to the finish line. It's as if you love her more than you love sex. But you can't abandon me, Ernst. You've got the boys to think about.

— My heart's with you, but our future's with *Suzuki*. Dita's a means to an end. That's all. Once we're in the West, she'll be a relic from the distant past. We'll be free.

— You'll be free? Free to race, maybe. But me? How'll I be free? Free to shop? Free to worry about you killing yourself on the track? Free to lose sleep? Free to raise our children without their father? I'm worried that the Stasi will break down our door in the middle of the night and shoot me in the head.

— You'll be free to live the life you chose when you married me. Life on a razor's edge. In the red zone. That's where I flourish, flying low. This is who I am. Who I have always been.

He poured them each a small drink.
— To Monza.
She drank her vodka down and reached for more.

32

Eine Mutter auf der Flucht
(A Mother on the Run)

Gerda reached for the bottle. With Ernst out of the house, Boris sleeping, and Olaf playing, she had some time to herself. She turned the radio on and hummed along with Nana Gualdi singing about the stupidity of love.

Then someone tapped on the door and Gerda nearly knocked the bottle over.

Olaf jumped up from his colouring and ran to open the door.

— Wait for me, honey. But she was too late.

Olaf pulled down on the handle and swung the door open.

— Dita, he squealed.

Struggling to her feet, Gerda felt dizzy. She clutched the back of the chair to steady herself.

— *Was macht sie hier* (What is she doing here)?

Gerda staggered down the hall.

Dita smiled at Olaf as he stood on her foot peg and hugged her tank.

Gerda pulled him off.

— *Lauf zurück zu deinen Farben, mein Sohn* (Run back to your colouring, my son). *Dita bleibt nicht lange* (Dita's not staying long).

— Please, Mum. I want to show her my new motorbike.

— You have a motorcycle?

— *Es ist eines* (It's one), den Papa mir von der Insel... mit gebraucht (that Dad brought me from the Isle of...).

— Man? Dita asked.

Bitte, Mama (Please, Mum), *lass Dita bleiben* (let Dita stay). *Ich werde Boris nicht wecken* (I won't wake Boris). *Das verspreche ich* (I promise).

Gerda sighed.

— All right, young man. Just for a few minutes.

— I'll be back, Dita. Don't leave.

She smiled and he ran to his room, rummaging through his things.

Gerda seethed. She stepped back from the door, allowing Dita to roll into the apartment.

— What's going on, Gerda? Your breath. Have you been drinking? It's not even ten in the morning.

— Don't play me the fool Dita. You're screwing Ernst, and you want me to stay sober? *Warum hast du mich betrogen* (Why have you betrayed me)?

— I've done nothing you haven't already agreed to.

— Exactly what are you talking about?

— When you married Ernst, you knew the score.

— It's one thing to know. But another to see your best friend...

— If I could undo that, I would. I regret crossing the line with Ernst, but I do not regret taking him over the finish line.

— Oh, please. For God's sake.

— You're here today because of what I have done for you. We are in this together.

Gerda shook her head. Angry.

— You're right but it pisses me off. At least let me wallow in my misery.

Boris woke up, bawling. Gerda lifted him out of his bassinet.

— Oh my, little man, you're riper than a dairy farm. She made a face and turned to Dita. I need to change his diaper. You better be gone when I return. She took her son to the nursery.

Olaf ran out of his room.

— Dita, I finally found it. Can you show me how to pop a wheelie?

Dita knelt on the floor and smiled.

— Olaf, *Ich würde fast alles für dich tun* (I'd do almost anything for you).

He hugged her, and they played motorcycle.

— You need to twist the throttle until the front wheel lifts. Not too much, though, or you'll flip backwards.

Olaf gunned it and the bike spun out of control.

Dita laughed.

— *Nicht so schnell, Liebling, nicht so schnell* (Not so fast, darling, not so fast).

Olaf tried again.

— That's right. Easy does it. Pretty soon, you'll be at the Nürburgring. She returned his hug, and he fell even more deeply in love with her.

Degner strode into the apartment, unaware of the (fe)maelstrom ahead of him. He saw Dita with his son.

— What are you doing here? Where's Gerda?

— Ernst I....

— Papa, you're home. Dita showed me how to pop a wheelie. Not too much throttle, she said.

Degner knelt.

— That's right, son. Just enough to pull the front wheel off the ground. It's a light touch, but you better keep the pressure on. Look where you're going. Don't get distracted.

Gerda entered the room.

— You're still here? She cast a withering glance at Dita. Then she saw her husband. Oh, you! She snarled.

He turned the volume up on the radio.

— Bad news.

— What do you mean?

— *Bitte*, (Pardon)? Dita asked.

— Petry can't make Monza. He pulled a crumpled telegram out of his pocket. See?

— Why? Does he give a reason?

— He couldn't get the air supply ready.

— What are you talking about? Olaf asked.

— Oh, nothing son, Degner replied. We're trying to find a better air breather for Dita. With the new engine, she's gasping at the top end. We're trying to increase her lung capacity.

— That must be magic, Papa!

— You're telling me!

Gerda took Olaf back to his colouring and made a pot of *Kräutertee* (herbal tea). Dita's right, she thought, her mind clearing. We're in this mess together. We need to find a way out. Tea might help. Fighting won't.

— *Unabhängig davon werde ich nicht zulassen* (Regardless, I'm not going to allow), *dass diese beiden Trottel mein Leben zerstören* (both these dimwits to destroy my life). *Ich bin derjenige* (I'm the one), *der alles verlieren wird* (about to lose everything).

Degner turned to Dita.

— Shouldn't you be going?

— Leave her alone, Ernst, Gerda said. The two of you have already caused enough trouble. Don't make matters worse.

— I'm here to make things right with Gerda. Have you seen the shape she's in?

— Shut up, Dita! Don't talk like I'm not here.

— Rolling towards the door, Dita said, I was a fool. Please forgive me.

— If you say sorry once more, I'll kick you down the stairs and tip you onto the road. Get back in here.

Gerda looked from Dita to Degner.

— At least she has the guts to make things right.

Dita rolled to the door.

— Dita! *Komm wieder rein* (You're not going anywhere). We need to sort this out. Whether we like to or not, we could lose everything.

— It didn't mean a thing, Ernst said. Dita means nothing to me.

— Don't lie to me, Ernst. Dita's brought you places I never could. *Du hast sie geliebt* (You've loved her), *solange ich dich kenne* (as long as I have known the two of you).

— Gerda, Dita said.

— Well, I love her too! Olaf exclaimed. He crawled up onto Dita's saddle with his colouring book in hand. You are really, really, really nice.

— A three-really-nice motorcycle? Degner asked Olaf. I'd give her a two, tops. Your Momma's the only three in my books.

Olaf smiled.

— *Du bist ein sehr süßer Junge* (You are a very sweet boy). *Ich liebe dich von ganzem Herzen* (I love you with all my heart).

— You have a heart?

— *Sogar ein Gehirn* (Even a brain)!

— Olaf! Now back to your room, Gerda said. We adults need to talk alone. When we're done, we can all go for ice cream.

— *Eis, wirklich* (Ice cream, really)?

Reluctantly, Olaf climbed down from Dita. He looked at his Mum.

— *Du versprichst* (You promise)?

— *Mit meinem ganzen Herzen* (With all my heart).

Olaf ran to his room and shut the door.

Gerda turned the volume louder.

— We can't live without Dita, Gerda said to Degner. We can't lose her. There are limits, though. Dishonesty will break us apart.

— Gerda, Ernst, Dita said.

She was caught in a No-Woman's Land where you are shot if you go forward or damned to Hell if you step back. There is no refuge in this in-between space—only landmines, exploding shells, and bullets aimed for the heart. Ordnance and one-night stands. If the one doesn't kill you, the other will rip you apart.

— *Im Kampf um die Liebe* (In the battle for love), *werden keine Gefangenen genommen* (no prisoners are taken). *Geiseln auch nicht* (no hostages either).

Degner looked at the two. He had nothing to say. Yeah, yeah, he fooled around with Dita. But so what? She's a motorcycle, and he's a racer. This is what he does. For God's sake, he races bikes for a living. He'll ride with the devil to win.

Degner knew that there was no way for him to stay in that apartment and live, so he did the only thing possible thing a man could do. He made a run for it.

— *Entschuldigung Sie, meine Damen* (Excuse me ladies). *Ich muss aufs Klo.* (I must use the loo).

He hurried down the hall and opened the door to Olaf's room.

— *Willst du auf ein Eis gehen* (Want to go for some ice cream)?

Olaf looked at this father.

— With Dita? His voice brightened.

— Nah. Just the two of us. We boys need to stick together.

He grabbed Olaf's hand and pulled him out of the apartment. They raced down the street.

— *Wohin gehen die Zwei* (Where are they going)? Dita looked at Gerda, dumbfounded. *Was sollen wir tun* (What shall we do)?

Gerda handed her a cup of tea.

— Let them go. You and I have some business to attend to first.

Dita sipped the herbal tea and made a wry face.

— Straight up's not my first choice. I need a mix.

Gerda smiled.

— It should calm your nerves, though.

— I do well when I'm hot and about to explode, Dita said. She put the cup down. This swill puts out my fire.

— We have to join forces, Gerda said. We can't depend on Ernst. He doesn't have our best interests in mind.

— He wants the *World Championship.* That's all that matters.

— He and Tom Phillis are neck and neck. It's a race too close to call. Who will win?

— Petry won't be ready for Monza, but he'll be set for Kristianstad. Of that I'm certain. We'll have to pack Ernst's bag, though. Make sure he doesn't forget anything.

— He must connect with Matsumiya and take the ferry to Denmark.

— How about asking Hartmann if Ernst could drive alone to Sweden?

— I could. Alfred has never said no to me.

— That way, we'll have a vehicle when we're settled. Once he makes it to safety, he could phone. Petry could give him a code word to know we've made it.

— I can do that, Dita said.

— The challenge is getting Ernst to carry through. He has a one-track mind these days. If he wins the Swedish *GP,* he'll be even more reluctant to abandon *MZ,* no matter how good *Suzuki*s offer is.

— We must keep him from backing out at the last minute. Once he senses victory is within his grasp, there's no telling who he'll betray.

— Do you have any ideas?

— As a matter of fact, I do. Maybe throw a mechanical at the last possible moment and force his hand.

— That's settled then. At least we're on the same page.

— Let's get Boris and catch up to those boys

— I bet Ernst is craving some *Fürst Pückler* (Prince Pückler) ice cream. There's a shop down the street. The queue might not be too long.

— The two of you better jump on.

Gerda grabbed Boris and wrapped him around her front with a long, wide, brightly coloured shawl. She hung a messenger bag filled with baby things over her back.

— Ready, she said.

— Bottles? Dita asked.

— I have my girls. They're ready when he's hungry. I'm learning to mother on the run.

— You know more than you think, Dita said as they sped off.

— Oh my, Gerda said, hanging on for dear life. *Du bist eine heiße, kleine Nummer* (You are a hot little number). *Kein Wunder, dass Ernst dich mag* (No wonder Ernst likes you).

33

Besondere Bitte
(Special Request)

Dita rolled into Alfred Hartmann's office. Once she was in, he shut the door and motioned her to the corner by the window, near a coffee table with some large books on it. The sun shone through the windows. He placed a piece of cardboard on the floor.

— If you don't mind?

— Honestly, Alfred, do you think this is necessary? I'm not British.

— It's just in case. I don't want Helga mad at me.

— Drip oil and stain your precious floor?

— Helga may be the cleaning lady, but she's an important part of my staff. A falling out with her would be disastrous.

— She's Berlin's eyes and ears on your operation?

— Exactly. And she doesn't know I know.

— Then this is our little secret.

— So, what's this about? Degner? Hartmann settled back into the sofa and lit a big Cuban cigar. I know I shouldn't, but these smokes are one of the few benefits living here has over life in America.

— Deg wants to drive his *Wartburg* to Sassnitz and take the ferry to Sweden by himself. It's his way of relaxing and prepping for the race.

— Always pushing the boundaries, that boy. We scrambled to survive when the *Engländer* bombed the Hell out of us. Now he's milking the system for all it's worth. Can't say I blame him. I'd do the same. Good thing he's a star.

— So, you'll let him?

— If I don't, he'll go sideways. Sweden's a neutral country, but the Stasi has a long reach. Besides, I'll be in Kristianstad.

— Gerda and I were talking. That's all. We want to do everything we can to ensure he wins this *GP*.

Hartmann took a long drag on his cigar.

— The numbers work. If Degner doesn't screw up, maybe Kaaden will finally have his *World Championship*.

— Driving on his own should settle his mind. Calm his nerves down.

— I want *Deutscher Fernsehfunk* (German Television Broadcasting) to air the race. Maybe get Erich Bergauer to give an on-air interview about *MZ* and Kaaden's achievements.

— Not *Onkel* Walter himself?

— Have you heard him drone on? We need someone who will hold the audience's attention. Not one who'll put them to sleep. The audience will love Bergauer. He's the best communicator on the *Rennkollektiv*. Everyone across the country will be watching.

— So, it's settled then? Dita asked.

— About Degner? Of course, he can have his taste of freedom. Gerda and the boys will be here waiting. He won't do anything to jeopardize their safety.

$$34$$

Zigaretten und Wodka
(Cigarettes and Vodka)

Paul Petry pulled the Lincoln up to the border control where the East German guards stood with their machine guns. Alsatians on long leashes waited for their masters' commands. Petry felt nervous but trusted his instincts. Besides, he knew these guards. They were familiar with him, or at least his car.

Its size, white wall tires, and huge V-8 engine caused quite a stir when he first travelled to Leipzig. Once it became a familiar sight, the guards took him for granted. They saw in Petry what they wanted to see: a wealthy West German with a large car and a trunk full of cigarettes.

Petry rolled down his window as he approached the front of the line.

— *Papiere!* The guard ordered.

Petry handed them over.

Another guard ogled the big car with his dog sniffing tires, fenders, front and back. When he finished, he returned to his master's side, waiting for a treat. He discovered nothing of interest in his search.

— Where are you going?

— The trade fair. I own a motorcycle shop in Saarbrucken that sells *MZs*. I'm meeting some government officials to make arrangements to increase my order. I can't get enough.

— Who's the best rider with *MZ*?

— Ernst Degner, of course. He has a real chance of winning the *World Championship* this year.

The guard returned the papers and looked at the dog handler.

— *Etwas* (anything)?

— *Nichts.*

— You may go. The guard waved him through.

Petry put the Lincoln into Drive and eased his way into East Berlin. Before he met with the Degners, he needed to exchange his cartons of cigarettes for a few cases of vodka.

35

Betäubungsmittel
(Mickey Finn)

— We better fill the tank up before we go any further, Gerda said, pointing to the petrol station on the corner. Stopping here won't raise any suspicions. You take Olaf to the toilet while I change Boris's diaper.

— Then we'll give the boys their drinks. Petry's just a few blocks from here. Once we arrive, they'll be sound asleep.

A few minutes later, they pulled into the darkened shadow of a still bombed-out building, a short drive from the entrance to the Transit Corridor. Degner parked beside Petry. The boys were sound asleep.

— You ready for this, Gerda? Petry asked as he gave her a quick hug.

— Once I have a swig, she said as she pulled out a flask. I'll sleep through anything.

— What about the boys?

— They're so knocked out; they won't make a peep.

— While Deg drove, I read *Struwwelpeter* to keep them from napping.

— That should do it, Petry laughed. Those stories scared me awake when I was a child.

— They still do me.

Petry and Degner unloaded the cases of vodka from the cavernous trunk. Petry pulled back the carpet and removed the false floor to reveal a well-padded compartment, spacious enough for one adult and two small boys.

— Try not to worry, Gerda. I made it big enough for Fidele. She's your size. There's even enough wiggle room if you need to stretch a bit. The air supply's good too. Don't panic.

— I get claustrophobic in small spaces. I can't breathe.

— Petry gave her a smoke. Have one of these. It'll calm your nerves.

She sucked back on the cigarette and returned it to Petry. He helped her into the compartment.

Degner held the sleeping Boris and gave him a peck before handing him to Gerda. She snuggled with her son, hardly believing what was happening. Petry nestled Olaf beside the two. Gerda put her hand on his chest and shut her eyes. The steady beating of his heart calmed her down.

— I'm doing this for them, she reminded herself. The future is theirs. She closed her eyes and took a few deep breaths before passing out. Petry pulled off her shoes and tucked her and the boys in with a blanket.

Degner handed Petry the false floor, which he fitted into place. He rolled the carpet back down and tucked in its edges. The compartment was now completely hidden.

— Here's my *MZ*. All torn apart and ready to be put back together again.

— That should deter the guards from unloading the entire vehicle.

He stowed the boxes as Degner handed them to him. A couple of the larger ones went on the back seat.

— After this trip, I'll have enough spare parts on my shelves for a year, Petry said.

Degner shut the lid and shook hands with Petry.

— Thanks for this.

— Good luck, Petry said.

— Just get my family through. I'll phone Fidele when I make it into West Germany.

Degner stepped into the shadows as Petry settled in the driver's seat, started the big V-8, and rumbled out onto the street, his rear signal blinking red.

Degner jumped into the *Wartburg* and cut into a lane of vehicles bearing down on him. He wove through the traffic, downshifted into the corner, and raced away from the corridor. As usual, he had to be in first place.

At the border control, Petry rolled to a stop. The guards saw the big Lincoln and smiled. They waved him through. No questions asked.

However, the car behind him wasn't so lucky. As the dogs approached the vehicle, they started to bark. The guards ordered the driver out.

36

Straßen aus Gold
(Streets of Gold)

Gerda awoke to a blinding light. She groaned and covered her eyes with her arm. Then she remembered where she was and panicked.

— *Meine Jungs, meine Jungs* (My boys, my boys).

She looked around, wildly afraid. She heard a voice in the background.

— *Du bist sicher* (You are safe). *Wir haben es nach Westdeutschland geschafft* (We've made it to West Germany).

— The boys are fine, Petry said. He tried to soothe her awake.

— Oh, God, oh God, she cried as she turned over and struggled up onto her knees. She shook Boris and then Olaf.

— *Verdammt, Ernst, verdammt* (Damn you Ernst, damn you), she swore. *Bitte Gott, meine Jungs* (Please God, my boys). *Aufwachen* (Wake up), she prayed.

They snuffled and began to cry. She sobbed with relief, gasping for air.

— Gerda, they're awake. You're safe. Let me help you.

She snagged her pantyhose when she crawled out of the trunk. Petry steadied her as she sat on a pile of boxes he had set on the ground. He handed her the squalling Boris and lifted the shrieking Olaf from the trunk. They clung to their mother and would not let her go.

Petry knelt and hugged all three.

— You're safe. We made it. You're in the West. You're free. There's nothing more to worry about.

Gerda pulled her dress down below her knees. She looked at the run in her nylons.

— Why hadn't I worn pants? Then she laughed. If that's the worst of my problems, I'll get by. She wiped the tears from her eyes.

She slipped on her shoes and grabbed Olaf's hand.

— Let's go to the car. I need to feed Boris. I bet you're thirsty too.

They sat in the back seat. Gerda gave Olaf a drink of water and a piece of chocolate.

— Eat this, she said. You'll feel better.

Petry busied himself, reloading the car.

After settling Olaf, she covered herself with a shawl and tried nursing Boris. Despite the comfort and intimacy that she shared with her son; she had no milk for him. The world kept crashing in. He bawled and bawled. She dug out a baby bottle with formula she had packed as a precaution. He latched onto it and suckled hungrily. Then he needed burping. She held him up and patted his shoulder blades. The air bubble escaped and suddenly all was right with the world. He smiled and burbled. He broke his mother's heart; he was so damned cute.

— Ernst, she said to herself, her thoughts racing. What have we done? How could we put our children in such danger? And for what? More money? A fancy car? What fools we are. And I encouraged you. I can't believe it.

She looked out on the rest area's parking lot adjacent to the Autobahn. The whine of high-powered automobiles and heavy truck tires filled the air. Heavy exhaust settled in the low areas, making it hard for her to breathe. She was suffocating.

While Gerda tended to her sons, Petry went to the payphone and called Fidele.

— Has Degner called? No? Good. Everyone here's fine. We crossed the border without a problem. Soon as Gerda is done with the boys, we'll be leaving for Saarbrucken.

He hung up and hurried back to the car.

— Hey, Olaf, Gerda said.

He was squeezing his legs together. Need to pee? I do.

He nodded his head. Gerda picked Boris up and slid out of the car. Olaf grabbed his mother's hand.

— We're off to the toilet, she said to Petry, who was just finishing up.

— I need to as well. At my age, you don't want to miss any opportunity. He hurried to the Men's while Gerda and the boys went to the Women's.

— Let's see if western toilets are any better than the ones back home, Gerda said.

— *Vielleicht sind sie mit Gold bedeckt* (Maybe they're covered with gold)?

— Just like this road?

They laughed like there was no tomorrow.

37

Feuerringe
(Rings of Fire)

— We are broadcasting from our studio at the Swedish *Grand Prix* in Kristianstad, the *Deutscher Fernsehfunk* announcer spoke into the camera. Today *MZ* will secure its hold on the *World Championship*. Ernst Degner can win if his teammates keep the Australian Tom Phillis to third place. Kristianstad is a fast track, but the *MZ* 125s are the quickest in their class. The weather conditions are perfect for an East German victory.

Images of the *MZ Rennkollektiv* filled the screen. Five 125s in their signature blue and silver colours stood gleaming in a row.

— After the race, the announcer continued, we'll interview Eric Bergauer, *MZ*'s chief engineer. He'll give us the insider's scoop on Degner's magnificent win.

At the track where the bikes were lined up, the riders went through their pre-race rituals of tightening the straps on their helmets, adjusting goggles, and pulling on gloves. They knew the winning combination and followed it precisely. Walter went through his formalities once more, checking the humidity, barometric pressure, and temperature. It was hot, hot, hot. He made certain the carburetors were set properly and that the technicians fitted the correct expansion chambers for the conditions.

The problem was that each change in altitude and barometric pressure necessitated a different length and shape of expansion chamber. It took experience and luck to fit the right pipe for the weather on race day. Sometimes one needed to be changed on the fly with the quick-release lever Walter designed.

— *Jetzt ist nicht die Zeit für mechanische Fehler unsererseits* (This is not the time for any mechanical lapses on our part). *Diese Motorräder müssen perfekt laufen* (These bikes have to run perfectly).

— Have you adjusted the carbs to accommodate the change in elevation, Dita badgered her favourite uncle. We're nearly at sea level, you know.

— I made that mistake once. At Assen, I know. Thanks for not letting me forget.

— Oh, I won't, don't you worry. Not that, anyhow.

The racers pushed their bikes out of the paddock and over to the track.

111

— Easy does it this time, Ernst, Dita said.

He smiled and gave her a bump start. Once the engine fired and warmed, he turned it off and rolled her to his position on the starting grid.

— I'm ready to take the title. I need a few more points to consolidate my win.

When the race started, the East German fans groaned as Tom Phillis, Jim Redman, Kuninitsu Takahashi, and Luigi Taveri on *Honda*s pulled ahead of Degner. Shepherd crashed by the end of the first lap , but all was not lost. Degner sped ahead of his nearest rival by three hundred metres. By the second lap, he was five hundred meters in the lead. He soon distanced himself from the rest of the pack. If Brehme kept Phillis out of second place, the championship would be his.

When rounding the last curve in the third lap, Dita's engine grew hotter and hotter.

— *Nicht so schnell* (Not so fast), she cried. *Etwas langsamer.* Ernst, *bitte.* (A little slower. Ernst, please).

She knew all too well that her cautioning would have its opposite effect.

For his family's sake, Degner needed to abandon the race, even with victory this close. He had to get on the road to the ferry. But he wouldn't if he was leading in the final stretch. Dita needed to do something. Now!

Get Degner to abandon the race, meet Matsumiya, and defect.

Gerda and the boys depended on him. They depended on her. There was no turning back. Dita had her work cut out for her. She needed Degner, in spite of his experience, to redline her engine.

Lingering oil smouldered in Dita's combustion chamber and thinned to a sheen on her cylinder wall.

— I can't slow down now, he said. To Hell with you. I need this win, so I can leave here victorious.

Degner's mind turned to the final stretch and the checkered flag. It was his and there was no stopping him.

He twitched and downshifted into the curve, and the engine rpm skyrocketed. As the steel piston rings burned through the oil residue in the heat, they warped and buckled, gouging red hot into the engine's soft-cast aluminum alloy. Then the piston stopped dead in mid-stroke. The engine seized, and the rear wheel locked.

Degner flew headfirst over Dita's handlebars at 140 km/h. He skimmed the pavement and hit the ground, bouncing, and tumbling into the air, up and down, up and over, again and again. The thin leather suit kept him from losing his skin. He slid into the sand and came to a stop in the grass, shaken, stirred, and bruised, but most importantly, not broken.

Heart racing, he wiggled his fingers and toes. All intact, he thought. Good. He struggled to his feet.

Aching, he looked around. Bikes screamed past.

That bitch Dita, pieces of her fairing scattered everywhere. He didn't care. She failed him, and now he'd lost the race.

It's all her fault, he said to himself. He staggered toward the pits. Kaaden can clean up the mess she made. I need to get out of here.

The track crew hurried to the scene of the accident. Medics with a stretcher followed close behind but Degner waved them off.

— Get that bike off the track before she causes any more harm.

Pushing his way through the on-lookers, he nodded to Matsumiya as he hurried to the hotel to get cleaned up. He popped a handful of painkillers. The *Wartburg* was packed and ready for the drive to the ferry.

38

Gangwechsel
(Shifting Gears)

— That's it, Eric? Walter asked. Are you off then?

— *Ja*, Bergauer said. It's no use me hanging around. Berlin cancelled the interview with state television. I need to see what went wrong with Dita.

— I'm worried about her. She's the best machine we have. Do what you can. We'll confer later this week.

— It sure makes you wonder, though, doesn't it? Why her engine seized in the corner? You don't think?

He raised his eyebrow.

— That Degner downshifted too early?

Bergauer nodded.

— Not intentionally, that's for sure. His mind must have wandered.

— But where? He's too experienced to lose focus.

— *Ich habe keines Ahnung* (I have no idea), Walter said, shaking his head.

— I better get going if I'm to make the ferry.

— When you come to port, it'll be dark. Spend the night in Sassnitz.

— Nah, I'll be fine. I've driven this road hundreds of times. There's nothing on it that'll surprise me. Besides, I'm eager to tear Dita apart and put her back together again. I have an idea about increasing her output for Argentina.

— We can talk about this later. You're always thinking ahead. Walter slapped his old friend on the shoulder. Drive safely, hear? The long road to Zschopau is jet-black at night.

39

Der rote Abendhimmel
(The Red Evening Sky)

Once the 250cc race was over, the 22-member *Rennkollektiv* made their way to the bar at the *Turisthotellet* (Tourist Hotel). They needed to drink and talk and sing songs long into the night.

— Where's Degner? Hartmann asked.

— Probably in his room, Walter said. He doesn't usually allow losses on the track to get him down. He's too resilient to need a drink right now.

— Best let him alone then, Hartmann said as he lit a cigar and looked at the setting sun. *Morgen wird es ein besserer Tag sein* (Tomorrow will be a better day). *Der Abendhimmel ist rot* (The evening sky is red).

40

Das dicke Ende
(Hell to Pay)

Just before he reached the approach to the ferry to Denmark, Degner pulled over to the side of the road. Matsumiya jumped out of the car behind him.

— You made it. That was quite the tumble. Are you okay?

— Just a little sore.

— Let's see what you have for me.

— And what you have for me.

Matsumiya pulled out an envelope filled with cash.

— Half now and the other half when you've built the 22-hp engine.

Degner opened the trunk and unclasped his suitcase. He shuffled some clothes aside and dug out a piston the size of a small cup, various engine parts, and the camera with several rolls of film.

— That's everything.

Matsumiya smiled and nodded. He handed the envelope to Degner and put everything into a cloth bag.

Degner thumbed through the thick wad of bills. Satisfied, he tucked the envelope in the corner of his suitcase.

— Mr. Suzuki will be pleased.

— I should think so. I've fulfilled my part of the bargain.

— So far, yes.

There was no love lost between the two men. They made a deal involving the exchange of cash for an underhanded deal. Plain and simple. Patriotism, good faith, and loyalty weren't part of the bargain. Each wanted all he could get out of the transaction. Betrayal bedamned. Cold hard currency was all that counted.

Degner shut the lid on the trunk, jumped into the car, and sped off down the road to the ferry.

Matsumiya returned to his car and did a quick U-turn. He needed to get back to Kristianstad before anyone suspected he was involved with Degner's disappearance. There'll be Hell to pay, but the later the better. He'd be getting a bonus on top of his fee.

He could hardly wait.

41

Asyl

(Asylum)

With the 1958 removal of passport checks at the border between Sweden and Denmark, Degner could drive directly to the West German border control near Handewitt. He pulled out his East German passport and gave it to the guard.

— *Ich bin gerade aus der DDR geflohen* (I've just fled East Germany) *Ich möchte Asyl* (I'd like asylum). *Meine Frau und meine Kinder sind schon hier* (My wife and children are already here). *Sie sind mit Freunden auf dem Weg nach Saarbrücken* (They're on their way to Saarbrucken with friends).

— *Park dein Fahrzeug dort* (Park your vehicle over there). *Komm mit mir* (Come with me).

Once inside a small room, the guard handed Degner a sheaf of forms to fill out and sign at the bottom.

— So, you're Ernst Degner, the famous motorcycle racer. I've been following your progress on the *Grand Prix*.

Once he finished, Degner handed the documents back to the officer.

— It looks like everything is in order. Where will you be living?

Degner gave him Paul Petry's address and telephone number.

— We'll be staying there until we find our own place.

— As soon as you arrive, report to the authorities, and register.

— Yes, sir. I will. He handed the guard a signed photograph.

With that, the officer stamped Degner's visa and allowed him to enter the country.

Degner headed south on the Autobahn. He could not stay up to speed in the left lane. Cars pulled behind him and flashed their lights, honking their horns. He pulled over to the right. Big *Mercedes* and *BMWs* roared past his *Wartburg*. Degner was grim-faced. He was not used to being left behind.

Wondering how Gerda and the boys fared in the trunk of Petry's car, he pulled off the Autobahn into a rest area. Better give them a call, he thought. He dug into his pocket for some change. All he had was a handful of East German coins.

— Sure hope they work, he prayed.

He dropped the coins into the slot. The phone's high- and low-frequency alternating current scanned and rejected them. They fell through the coin chute into the refund box below.

He couldn't complete his call and cursed that damned Petry for not thinking about this. He returned to his car and drove in the slow lane all the way to Saarbrucken.

Gerda was frantic and worried sick. Where was he? What happened? Why hasn't he called.

It was the longest night of her life.

42

Der Morgen danach
(The Morning After)

The following day, the *MZ* team members met for breakfast. They piled their gear in the lobby, so they could board the bus after eating. Mechanics, racers, and engineers lined up together, happily chatting, eager to enjoy the famed Swedish smorgasbord. They were like family and jostled each other as they filled their plates with bread, cheese, cold cuts, cured salmon, and boiled eggs. And the coffee, of course, the delicious Swedish *fika* that was unlike anything they'd ever get back home.

—Has anyone seen Degner, Hartmann asked, doing a headcount.

— Not since he left the track yesterday.

— I'll see if he slept in, Musiol said, and he sprinted up the stairs.

He returned immediately and raised the alarm. Brehme ran out to the parking lot and discovered that the *Wartburg* was missing.

Hartmann hurried to the hotel telephone, and Walter ordered everyone on the bus. They stowed their bags, found their seats, and left for Zschopau, grim-faced and worried.

43

Ein anderer Weg
(Another Way)

When they arrived back in Zschopau late that night, the *Rennkollektiv* heard the bad news about Eric Bergauer during his drive down the highway. He had run into the unlit back of a transport truck that had stalled in the middle of the lane. He was alive but suffered a catastrophic head injury. Dita was tossed about but stayed intact. For her, there was nothing Kaaden couldn't fix. For Bergauer, however, it was the end of his old life and the beginning of something new.

— Schick*en Sie lieber jemanden* (You better send someone), *der sein Fahrzeug nach Zschopau zurückbringt* (to haul his vehicle back to Zschopau), Hartmann barked into the telephone.

— You, Hartmann said, pointing to Walter. Come with me. If you had anything to do with this, so help me God. We'll know soon enough.

He opened the back door to an unmarked vehicle with two Stasi officers in the front seat. Walter stepped in and Hartmann closed the door. The driver sped off and Hartmann followed close behind.

When they arrived at the Stasi headquarters on *Ruschestraße*, the two men shoved Walter through the doors and locked him in a cell.

— Let him stew. I'll talk to him in a bit. Any word on Degner?

— Just heard he's asked the West Germans for asylum. No word on his family yet.

— Shouldn't be too long until they show up. Wonder who helped them?

— Maybe that Petry? He's been quite cozy with the Degners.

— Send someone to Saarbrucken to find out what he's been up to, besides showing off his fancy American car.

Hartman and the Stasi interrogated Walter for four days, alternating good cop and bad cop, before determining that he did not know anything about Degner's defection.

— You're free to go, Hartmann said. However, our hopes of winning the *World Championship* are over. This may be all Degner's doing, but Berlin blames you and me entirely. We're finished.

— Perhaps there's another way, Walter said. I have an idea.

— What's that? Hartmann asked. He was angry but curious. He needed to salvage something from this nightmare.

— The International Six Days.

— Do we have a chance?

— Of course, Walter said. All of my riders can handle the tools and win any race they enter. They could dominate the field and show the world we can compete with the best.

— We better let this fiasco settle down. Then we'll see.

44

Offenes Haus
(Open House)

The front door opened and Fidele Petry stepped inside. She was tanned, well-rested, and more beautiful than ever after her four-week vacation on the *Côte d'Azur*.

For some inexplicable reason, Paul sent her off on her own, urging her to take a much-needed holiday. He had too much work to do with the Continental Circus going on full blast. He promised to make it up to her when she returned.

In the end, she stopped trying to convince him to join her. She invited some girlfriends along and had the time of her life. Sometimes husbands can be such a bore.

Fidele hadn't a clue what was going on or what Paul had been up to while she was away. Now the street outside her house was in an uproar. Journalists camped on the sidewalk, and newspapers were full of headlines about Degners' defection.

And here they were, the Degners, she couldn't quite believe her eyes, inside her house.

— Paul? What's all this?

Degner was on the telephone, trying to enter the last 125cc race of the 1961 season. He was this close to winning the *World Championship*. He was desperate to compete in the Argentina *GP*. Please God, please, he pleaded.

Gerda was sitting on the sofa feeding Boris, and Olaf was on the floor, playing with his motorcycles.

Fidele saw that this was a family in crisis and needed her help.

— I didn't want you caught up in this, Petry said. In case things went south.

— You should have warned me, Paul. This is unfair, me not knowing.

— I wanted to protect you. In case I was arrested, and you were interrogated. The less you knew the better. Or so I thought.

He helped her with her coat and carried her things to their bedroom.

Fidele hurried across the floor into the living room.

— Frau Degner, it's good to meet you. Are you okay?

Gerda smiled back.

— Yes, I'm fine, thank you, Frau Petry. Fidele sat down beside her.

— The worst is over, Gerda said. Now we must find a place of our own. We couldn't have done this without your husband's help. He saved my family, and I'm forever indebted to him.

Fidele smiled.

— As soon as our apartment is available, we'll be out from under your feet. Gerda was worried that the Stasi would burst through the door. She was anxious about overstaying her welcome in a stranger's home.

— You can stay here for as long as it takes. What is mine is yours.

— I don't want to be a burden. You and Paul have done enough for us.

— Don't worry about that. You and your boys are safe, and that's all that matters. She took a pack of cigarettes out of her purse and offered one to Gerda, but she declined.

— I'm trying to quit. The last few months have been murder. I need to stop before they kill me.

Degner's voice on the telephone grew louder. He was excited.

— That's such good news, Dr. Ehrlich. Riding your *EMC* at the Argentine *GP* will be just fantastic.

The women stopped to listen.

— Gerda and I will be at Brands Hatch this coming weekend. I'm to wave the Union Jack at the start of the race. I could stop by your shop to get the bike fitted. I'll need one of your mechanics to move the shifter to the left side of the gearbox for me. I can't get used to the English way of changing gears with the right foot.

Olaf fidgeted and fussed.

— Mama, Papa, can I go out to play?

— I don't think so, son. There are too many reporters out there.

— Who? Olaf insisted. Suddenly every bone in his body was aching. There was no relief from his growing pains. He had to get outside and burn off some energy. Now.

— Papa, he groaned. *Können wir jetzt in den Park gehen* (Can we go to the park now)? *Ich langweile mich. Bitte!* (I'm bored! Please!)

— Not now son, Gerda tried to shush him. Papa's on the phone. We need to stay put.

Olaf wailed, Boris howled, and Degner could hardly hear Joe Ehrlich.

— You don't say? Will Minter be there as well? He'll blow the competition out of the way. Your bikes are as fast as ours. I mean *MZs*.

Olaf's cries were growing louder and louder.

— I better hang up, sir. My son's getting difficult, being cooped up all the time. See you next week.

He cast a withering glance at Gerda and hurried down the hall. He needed some peace.

Degner brushed past Petry, who was returning from the bedroom.

— Anyone care for a drink? I sure could use one.

45

Zweite Chance
(Second Chances)

Walter tore small pieces from the thick slice of bread he had hewn from the loaf of rye on the cutting board.

— Your home cooking, he said. It's been too long.

He dropped the bread into the chicken dumpling soup Inge placed in front of him.

— Eat up, she said. You need to get your strength back. You've been through a lot.

— I'm a fool, Inge. I didn't suspect a thing. Walter slurped his soup.

— Not so quickly. It's hot. And you're not a fool. You have all the time in the world.

— You don't think Ernst did anything dishonest, do you? He spooned some of the dumplings into his mouth.

— What do you mean?

— He didn't just disappear, did he?

— Has something gone astray?

The idea made Inge put down her washcloth and look Walter straight in the eye.

— Do you think that he may have stolen something?

— Not sure. But what I now know for certain is that he has only his self-interest at heart. I wouldn't be surprised if he did something underhanded. Walter handed Inge the empty bowl. He was like a son to me. How could he?

— *Freunde und Familienmitglieder* (Friends and family members), *nicht nur völlig Fremde* (not just complete strangers), *verraten oft diejenigen, die ihnen am nächsten stehen* (often betray those closest to them).

— Not Ernst. He wouldn't. I gave him every opportunity to succeed.

— Well, you better get to the shop and check if anything's disappeared.

— I just hope that Matsumiya didn't put him up to something we'll all regret.

Walter hurried out the door and started the old 50cc *DKW* he had stored in the shed. He had rescued it from a neighbour and had been tinkering on it from time to time. The bike needed saving, and Walter couldn't bear to leave it abandoned.

— It's my calling. I can do no other. I restore old things.

— *Our Father of the Broken Down and Cross-Wired.*

Inge gave him a quick kiss on the cheek.

— You are full of grace. *Motorräder und Männer* (Motorcycles and men), *sie sind deine Kirche* (they are your church).

She gave the motorcycle tank an affectionate rub.

— This one's mine, she told her Walter. I claim it as my own.

He bump-started the grateful bike and rode down *Lindenweg* towards the factory.

— *Dies ist mein Tag, alter Mann* (This is my day, old man), the bike boasted.

— *Und meiner* (And mine), Walter replied. *Ich muss etwas Nützliches tun* (I need to do something useful).

— It's good to take me for a ride then. Fast, or slow, I don't care. Let the good times roll. Hard times, I pray, come again no more.

— *Wir sind zusammen dabei* (We're in this together).

— Inge too? The bike asked, his bike rising as Walter sped up a hill.

— Inge too, Walter replied.

When they arrived at the shop, Walter pulled up to a spot near the door and turned the engine off.

— Don't worry, *Schlingel* (Rascal). I'll be back.

The bike straightened up and cooled down.

— Papa, he assured Walter, I'm not going anywhere without you. Unless of course Inge shows up. Then there's no guarantee. I claim her as my one and only.

When Walter entered the shop, Dita looked up at him.

— It's about time, Nuncle! Where the Hell have you been? What's that you've been riding? I can smell his stale petrol from here. My oh my. You reek.

— Shut up, Dita. It's an urchin that needed rescuing. You'd do the same if you had opposable thumbs. Besides, he's in love with Inge.

Dita didn't reply as he began shuffling through files, papers, and drawers.

— What are you looking for? Maybe I can help.

— Look, Dita, do you think Degner took anything with him when he ran off?

— Like what?

— I'm not sure. I have a bad feeling. That's all.

— He spent a lot of time in the shop prior to Kristianstad.

— Working on his racer, I thought. Where is it, by the way? Walter looked around.

— Soon after finishing, he dismantled the entire thing and Petry hauled it away. I never asked why. It didn't occur to me. I assumed he took it home.

— Home? To his apartment in Karl-Marx-Stadt? That seems unlikely.

Walter dashed through the shop, looking in various nooks and crannies, noticing that the lads hadn't picked up a broom in days.

— Well, it's not here. And neither are those freshly cast pistons with the new alloy.

— Gone or misplaced?

— Nobody misplaces anything in my shop, Dita. It's too well-organized. Everyone here is trained to put tools back when they are finished.

— I know. I know. I know. "So, you can find them when you want them." As if I haven't heard that a thousand times before.

The thought that Degner had not only betrayed them, but that he had sold *MZ* out to *Suzuki* dawned upon both Walter and Dita. No, Degner, not that, they both feared.

— That Matsumiya. He was always around. Petry, too. I knew Ernst wanted to defect.

— And you didn't think to tell me?

— His discontent was obvious to everyone. I assumed you knew. He was always complaining about the raw deal he had been given. And that he had better soon be receiving a pay raise, or else. But I had no idea he'd steal your work and sell it to *Suzuki*.

Walter sat on a tall stool near the workbench and lit a cigarette.

— *Was sollen wir jetzt tun* (What should we do now), Dita?

— What we've always done. Make do. Concentrate on the races we can enter. *Suzuki* may have your old plans, but they don't have your latest idea. You must have something new in mind. Am I right?

— There is something I've been mulling over. Maybe we could get Alan to ride for us.

He pulled the calendar off the wall and flipped through the 1962 *Grand Prix* racing schedule. 15 July Solitude. 19 August Sachsenring. 23 September Tampere.

— It's a pity we won't be returning to the Isle of Man. It's such a glorious motorcycle race. Going 160 km/h on a public road. Pavement, cobblestones, lanes bordered with stone walls, hairpin turns, sheep in pastures, hay ricks on pathways, spectators an oil slick away, high mountain climbs, vistas, and plunging descents.

— Berlin might let us race in West Germany and Finland but not the *TT*.

— Alan will be there. So will that doll Mike Duff. Maybe even Hailwood.

— *Die Insel Man ist die Geschichte meines Lebens* (The Isle of Man is the story of my life). *Ich hätte fast den Höhepunkt erreicht* (I was about to reach the pinnacle). *Dann drehte sich das Glücksrad um* (Then whoosh, Fortune's Wheel turns). *Jetzt bin ich wieder down* (Now I'm back down).

— Get off it, Walter. Your life isn't over yet. You've suffered a blow. But you aren't dead. If you're breathing and have your wits about you, you can still make a difference.

— How?

— Figure it out! You don't have the right to feel sorry for yourself. You have the second half of your life ahead of you. You aren't crippled or brain dead. Don't squander the life you've been given.

— Life in the shadows, then? On the sidelines?

— It could be a lot worse. It could be Siberia. You should be grateful.

— As bad as it is, you're right. It's just that I'm getting old. I don't know how much more that I can handle.

— Well, you don't have much choice. You can't retire now. *Tante* Inge certainly won't be making your lunch at noon time. You'll have to scramble your own eggs. Get out your tool bag. You have bolts to remove. Modifications to make. *Mein Gott*, look at your hands. They're lily white. No wonder you're unhappy.

— Fifteen July at Solitude outside Stuttgart, you say? That should give me enough time to improve your chances of winning. I have an idea in mind.

— Next time I race, I want to fly outside the red zone.

46

Das Beste, was ich tun konnte
(The Best I Could Do)

In Saarbrucken, Petry opened the door to a cramped apartment and stepped back. He let the Degners enter first.

— *Dies ist das Beste* (This is the best), *was ich so kurzfristig für Sie tun kann* (that I could do for you on such short notice).

They looked around the suite in stunned silence. The place was smaller than the living room they had left behind in Karl-Marx-Stadt.

— *Die Toilette ist gleich den Flur entlang* (The toilet is down the hall), Petry pointed out the door.

He then bid Degner and Gerda adieu and left them to sort out their new life in the West. He did all he could for them. Now he had to save his marriage and get his business back on track. He wouldn't be crossing into East Germany for any more spectacular *MZs*.

Once he got down to the street, he hurried to his car. As he stepped into his vehicle, he looked behind him and thought he saw someone duck into a doorway. At that moment, he became afraid for his life and wondered why he put Fidele in such danger. He hoped she would be safe when he got home.

Back in the apartment, Gerda opened the kitchen cupboards and burst into tears.

— This will have to do for now, Degner said. Once I return from Japan, we'll look for something bigger and closer to your family.

— In the meantime?

— You'll have to make do.

Degner left Gerda and the boys alone in the apartment and hurried out. A wave of embarrassment hit him when he thought about the dump that Petry had found for them.

A Stasi officer in the shadows across the street took several photos of Degner and disappeared into the crowd.

Degner felt like a complete fool. Matsumiya took him for a ride and there was no turning back.

47

In Rauch

(Up in Smoke)

— That charlatan, Dita said. How could Ehrlich give Degner an *EMC* to ride in Argentina? He's using your work to grind us into the ground. I'll never forgive him.

— I needed the parts he had to offer when I sold him the bike. And he needed the expertise that I had to trade.

— It was a case of necessity coming to terms with opportunity, Hartmann said. With what we have on Degner, he won't be going far. Time is on our side.

Hartmann peered out the window through the smoke of the cigar he was puffing.

— Those damn Cubans sure know how to roll their tobacco. Walter, have you ever smoked a *Montecristo*?

— Can't say I have. They are a luxury I cannot afford.

— Well here, give this one a try. It'll change your life. Hartmann opened the cigar box on his desk and offered one to Walter. The smoke will cleanse your soul. How about you, Dita?

— Don't be ridiculous, Alfred. The only smoking I do is on the track. And it is a prayer for victory. Out of my tail and straight up to Heaven. I refuse to smoke cigars with the devil.

— But I'm not the devil, Dita. Just a man who keeps his feet on the ground. No matter what.

She looked out the window and saw another cloud scud by.

Walter cut the tip off, lit a match and held the burning flame close to the cigar. He drew back until the end glowed as red as Hell. With the cigar finally lit, he relaxed in his chair and savoured the smoke.

— I believe you're right, Herr Hartmann. The world is looking better than it has for a long time. We have to figure this out.

— Cigar smoke as incense, Dita said. All we need now is an indiscretion of priests to swing the *Botafumeiro* in the cathedral.

— Except we live in socialist East Germany where human effort is earthbound. We serve the here and now, not the there and then. This unholy smoke leads to a paradise that is available to the living, not just the dead.

— And the ash that forms on the tip? The butt end of your days? From ash to ash, this material world? Where our bright lives soon pale in darkening night?

— We are priests on an altar of our own making, Hartmann said. We make and unmake our destinies. God has nothing to do with it.

— Herr Hartmann, God or not, Walter said. We both share the blame for *EMC*'s success.

— Not that I would ever confess to such a crime against the State. Besides, what proof do you have?

— None whatsoever.

Walter took a another pull on his cigar.

— It's not as if I had any choice. Gear was on my mind, not absolution. I needed shocks, *Girling* rear suspension, *Amal* carbs, and *Lucas* ignition. But Ehrlich refused my Ostmarks. So, I traded what I had. Knowledge is money.

— I squeezed as much out of Berlin as I could for you, Hartmann said.

— Without lining your pockets, Dita said. Without feathering your nest? That's the rumour, you know.

— I took no more than what was expected of me, Dita. *MZ* was never shortchanged on my account.

— We needed to circumvent the embargo against East Germany. We did what we had to. How else were we to achieve the targets Berlin set for us?

— All I know is that when you cut a shady deal, you eventually pay for it, Dita said. The truth always comes out.

— The old men in Berlin are out for blood, Hartmann said. Degner has completely embarrassed them and put us all in jeopardy. The *East German National Motorcycle Racing Association* has revoked Degner's international licence. That should set him back.

— Except, only *FIM* can do that. Our association doesn't have the authority. It deals with national licences only.

— But do the Argentines know that? All we need is for them to get lost in the paperwork for a few days.

— The smoke and mirrors of bureaucracy, Dita said. Germans are the masters of that. East or West, the devil is in the red tape.

— And if the South Americans aren't fooled?

— Trans-Atlantic shipments are delayed all the time. We have ways and means with connections worldwide and in every industry. For the right price, someone could ensure that a certain securely packaged crate doesn't make it on the plane in time for its flight to Buenos Aires.

— And if it arrives on time, unpacked, everything in order? And Ernst wins?

— We protest to *FIM*. Degner is guilty of breaching his contract with *MZ*. And that is actionable. We have a case and he'd be fined. And maybe have his points revoked.

— When would that take place?

— Before the end of the year.

— He'll be in Japan by then, holed up with *Suzuki.* Doing whatever they want. The bastard!

48

Allein Essen

(Eating Alone)

Matsumiya and Degner were in *Suzuki* 's state-of-the-art workshop. Degner couldn't believe how modern it was compared to *MZ*s sorry excuse back in Zschopau. They stood well back from the technician who was using a dynamometer to measure the output on the engine Degner had built as part of his contract.

— After the collapse of the cotton market in the early 1950s, we had to find a new way to survive. The poverty of the post-war period ruled out producing luxury consumer goods. We needed something practical to transform our company's fortunes and enable our customers to provide for their families. Then we came up with an idea. Clip-on two-stroke gas engines for bicycles. Cheap, easy to maintain, and useful for everyday life. Soon we were selling 6,000 a month.

When the dynamometer measured 20 horsepower, everyone in the workshop cheered and congratulated Degner for a job well done. The technician reached for the *Kill* switch, but Degner stopped him. When it reached 24 hp, he looked at Matsumiya.

— Happy?

— Very.

Degner nodded and the technician turned the engine off.

— I'll have Accounting prepare a cheque for you.

— I have another idea for Mr. Suzuki. One that might guarantee a *GP* win. Care to pass it on?

— Of course! Matsumiya gave Degner his full attention. What is it?

— That we design a 50cc racing engine. There's less competition in that classification. The 125 and 250s are filled with heavy weights. With a 50, we'd have a greater chance of winning the 4 June *TT.* Then *Suzuki*'d have a fast, affordable motorcycle to add to its roster. They go 130 km/h.

— And if Mr. Suzuki agrees? Are you prepared to pay the cost?

— And that is?

— Eating raw fish in Hamamatsu for another month or so?

— Just not during Red Tide. I'd do anything to get back racing. I need to win.

— What about Mrs. Degner and the boys?

133

— They're fine. Gerda has a line on a larger place near her family. We were just waiting for this cheque.

— It's in the mail, Matsumiya said, laughing.

49

Unsere Frau des TT
(Our Lady of the *TT*)

On 4 June 1962, Alan Shepherd and the Canadian *GP* racer Mike Duff were near the starting line at the Isle of Man *TT*. Duff was carrying his trademark white helmet with the yellow maple leaf painted on its front.

— Alan, have a look at this! Duff grabbed Shepherd's arm. Who is that?

— What? Shepherd looked back to the start line.

— The blonde! My God, it's a woman astride an *Itom*!

— Yeah, so?

— Who is she?

— Haven't you heard? Beryl Swain, housewife and supermarket manager. She's Britain's fastest female motorcyclist.

— But racing solo on the Snaefel? Is that possible? A woman at the Isle of Man?

— Not impossible, Shepherd said. But highly improbable.

— I never thought I'd live to see it. A woman on the Continental Circus. That's my dream, you know?

— That'll be a great coming out day. But are you ready for the backlash?

— Gonna take some time. Guess I better screw my courage to the sticking place.

— Mrs. Swain's not the first female motorcycle racer, you know. Remember that German Inge Stoll? She raced here with her partner Jacques Drion in 1954 when the Sidecar *TT* was reintroduced. Came in fifth on the Clypse course. Then she broke her handhold in the 1957 *TT* and didn't finish. When she crashed in 1958 in Brno at the Czech *GP*, she died instantly.

— Oh, God, Duff said. And Drion?

— Succumbed a day later. She was 28 and he was 37.

— What a sorry turn of events. And her family?

— No children. Just her parents.

— Their only child?

Shepherd nodded.

— That's a bitter thing for any parent to endure.

— Now it's Mrs. Swain's turn to defy the odds. Except she's riding solo, not as a monkey in a sidecar, a counterweight hurtling down the road.

— Performing Giselle's *Dance of Death*? But without a happy ending. A tragedy in leathers and a helmet.

— A public relations nightmare more like. The *TT*'s too dangerous for women, they say.

— What about the hundreds of men already dead and gone? Maimed and hurt?

— It's much more telling when a beautiful young woman dies on the track. The weaker sex and all. The desire of men. The future of all mankind. Race officials are afraid she'll be killed on the Mountain course.

— And those women who survived both wars? Who fought battles behind enemy lines. They worked at the front and shouldered the burden back home. They lived in dangerous times and suffered unspeakable loss. They got on with it. Women are just as capable.

— And just as competitive. We cannot deny them their destiny. On the track or in the shop.

— Too bad about Tom Phillis crashing at Laurel Bank in the second lap of the 350.

— Who would have thought his number would come up? His ashes are to be scattered at the Start Line.

— And Mrs. Swain? She's braver than I. Knowing all this and coming out on her own. The pressure she's under.

— She does have her husband, Eddie, prepping her bikes. He's her grease-monkey.

— But is he merely indulging her dream? Thinking it'll pass once she gets it out of her system?

— I hope not, for the sake of their marriage. For the sake of her life.

— She causes quite the stir whenever she's on the roster. People want to see her. She's a Continental Circus attraction. But probably more of a sideshow than the main event. A piece of entertainment. No factory will ever offer her a contract. She has no future in her chosen endeavour. Imagine what that's like for her.

— Always a privateer with never quite enough money to make ends meet.

— A hopeless cause for a woman in a man's world, Duff said. She'd have an easier time if she changed sexes. At least then, she'd have a life worth living. The racetrack has no place for her. The race officials raised the minimum weight requirement to disqualify her.

— She's tiny.

— I saw her eating a huge order of fish and chips the other day, the only woman I've ever met trying to gain weight, not lose it.

— She knows how to handle a bike.

— Eddie owns a repair shop in Walthamstow. He's the one who got her into racing. Probably for the advertising, so he could sell more bikes to women. Increase his market share.

— She competed at Brands Hatch and Snetterton. Rode the 500 at Hackney Wick. But her specialty is the 50cc.

— What an ideal bike for female riders. Those little buggers can fly.

— Over 80 mph when they're tuned up. Small enough for a woman to ride and hoist from the ground when they tumble, which all riders do, eventually.

— And she's racing against Degner? Does she have a chance?

— Won't come close, but that's not the point. She's the one pushing boundaries. She's the one making the difference. This race is hers, regardless of who comes in second. She's the one making history.

— But only if someone keeps her story alive.

— What she's doing beggars the imagination, defying society's expectations, and being true to herself.

— I'd like to do that one day.

— Me too, brother. Me too.

50

Feuerball
(Fireball)

Pushing hard on the handlebars, Frank Perris, a Canadian-born British racer on contract with *Suzuki*, jumped side saddle onto the seat of his new 250cc four-cylinder RZ63. He popped the clutch, twisted the throttle, and the engine came to life. While the bike accelerated, he shifted the weight on his hip and slid his lower body into the riding position. With both feet on the pegs, legs tucked in close to the blistering hot engine, chest down on the fuel tank, arms close to his side, he craned his neck up, crooked, and painful, to look through the tiny windshield.

For whatever reason, the engine had failed when the Starter signaled the beginning of the race. Perris had done everything the way he'd done it a thousand times before.

Put the bike in first gear. Let out the clutch. Roll backwards until the engine is in the compression stroke and the bike stops. Get off. Engage the clutch. Squeeze the front brake and push hard on the handlebars. Release the brake at the Starter's signal, sprint forward, jump side saddle onto the bike, let out the clutch, twist the throttle as soon as the engine catches, slide into racing position, and peel off to win another championship.

But not this time.

The engine faltered and cost Perris seconds in a race where wins are made in thousandths.

Then the engine caught.

When he was up to speed, the pack was out of sight. He and Degner were there to win first and second place on the *Honda* Test Track at Suzuka. They wanted to prove that *Suzuki's* new bikes were better than anything *Honda* had to offer.

Then Perris rounded a bend. He saw a rider tumbling and bouncing off the pavement. The body landed, prone and unmoving, face down in a pool of flaming gasoline and oil. Thick gobs of black smoke fouled the air with the smell of scorching human flesh. Perris braked hard, the front and rear wheels locked, burning rubber, and screaming to a stop.

Race Marshalls pulled the lifeless body out of the flames and sprayed it with an extinguisher. It was his partner Degner, unconscious, the skin on his face bubbling from the burns, the rest of his body protected in leathers.

Perris gagged.

— Oh my God, oh God. Not Ernst, not this.

Medics scooped the unconscious body off the track and hurried to the ambulance. Perris couldn't race anymore. Winning was the last thing on his mind. He abandoned his bike and lurched back to the pits. Somehow, he made his way to the hospital Burn Unit.

Having won the 125cc race earlier that day, Perris stayed by Degner's side until he recovered enough to be shipped to Stuttgart, where he underwent months of skin grafts and plastic surgery. Back in West Germany, Degner would be close to Gerda and their children, but here in Japan, it was just the two of them, foreigners in a bewildering land.

The days were terrible, and the nights worse. Degner had to heal. He had to get those bandages off. The sooner the better. He didn't care what was underneath. All he wanted was to win.

He had to get ready for the 1964 season. He dreamt of nothing else. He had to get out of this god-damn bed and back on his bike.

Loaded on morphine, he could hardly shit. Oh God, the pain.

Had to.

There's nothing else.

— *Ich kann nichts anderes machen* (I can do no other), he told Matsumiya.

— You can't race at Daytona, Matsumiya replied. You're still in bandages.

— The Hell I won't. *Wenn ich es nicht tue* (If I don't), *werde ich sterben* (I'll die).

Part Four

51

Einladung
(Invitation)

Alan Shepherd slurped his tea, a blend that his wife Anne made of *Brooke Bond's Taj Mahal* and *Red Label*. They called it Two-Stroke.

— That's a good cuppa, Alan said as he scraped some butter across a cold slice of toast and slathered it with Medium-Cut Bitter Orange marmalade.

— That stack should keep you satisfied for a bit. I'm not sure how you can eat as much as you do and still be skinny enough to qualify for racing.

— I need to keep my weight up, dear. Going over has never been a problem. At least in the Regs, but you already know that. He grabbed another piece. I'd hate to be accused of taking advantage of the larger blokes on the track. The lighter the rider, the faster the bike. That's why the race officials have scales. To check the minimums.

— It's just not fair, she said, putting a kettle of water on their old *Aga* cooker. I starve myself to keep this figure and you eat everything in sight.

Anne Shepherd was a wisp of a woman who loved her rose garden more than her husband. She kept it in top shape, deadheading blossoms, pruning canes with a vengeance, trimming stems, loosening the soil, and digging fertilizer into the beds. She knew gardening as well as Alan knew carpet-laying, the trade that supported them before he turned pro. It kept her mind off his motorcycling. The roses bloomed with her worry and care. They flourished in her anxiety.

Quite frankly, she wasn't sure how much more she could handle. Worry takes its toll, and she'd had her fill of near misses. They'd been lucky so far, but for how much longer? Everybody's number comes up. It's just a question of when. Then there's a lifetime of suffering that follows one disappointment after another.

These thoughts have always given her pause. She's never been sure if she was quite up to the challenge that this marriage had thrust upon her.

The Shepherds were at their home in Grange-over-Sands, Lancashire, a picturesque town on the southern tip of the Cartmel Peninsula. Between the mountains and the sea near the Lake District in northwest England. It would have been a great place to retire if Alan weren't so hell-bent on winning a *World Championship*.

An unholy grail filled with suffering and woe, Anne thought bitterly.

In the meantime, she prodded him to get his gear together for the long drive to the London Airport. He might as well push off so that she could get on with her gardening.

The *gallica officinalis* near the gate needed tending. It was her pride, the Red Rose of Lancaster. Just yesterday, she noticed that some dead areas of its canes were varying in colour. I better keep my eye on them, she thought. I don't want any cankers to develop. She also had a *rosa alba*, the White Rose of York. That was Alan's joy on the other side of the gate. It wasn't quite so finicky.

— All packed? she asked.

Anne scalded the Brown Betty with boiling water from the kettle and added some to the thermos.

— So far, I've got my leathers, helmet, and tool bag. What else?

Once the kettle was back to a boil, she emptied the now warmed teapot, spooned in the loose black leaves, added the water, and gave it all a quick stir before slipping on the cozy.

— Gloves and goggles?

— They're already in the van.

— How about a change of underwear? Hate for you to end up wearing a pair of dirty shorts to the Emergency.

She emptied the hot thermos and added some milk.

— Oh right, I suppose a clean set of clothes would be a good idea. He raced to the bedroom, grabbed a few things from his dresser drawer, and stuffed them into his vintage World War II ditty bag.

Anne gave the pot another quick stir before pouring the tea into the thermos and tightening the stopper.

— Thanks. He put the thermos in the bag along with the sandwiches Anne wrapped in wax paper.

— You won't be spending all your time in the paddock.

— That's true. Maybe I'll see an orange grove. Pick a few to bring home. Could you imagine?

— To be honest? I can't imagine picking oranges fresh from a tree, or you in Daytona without me. I've always wanted to visit Florida. Maybe someday. The two of us. Palm Trees. Beaches. Cape Canaveral.

— You mean Kennedy.

— What? They changed the name already? Poor Jackie, what she and her children are going through. I can't imagine. Will she ever get over what happened?

— She'll get by like the rest of us. What begins at dawn ends at dusk. It's the in-between hours that count. Make do or fall behind.

— That seems a little harsh.

— But its true. Whether you're rich or poor, you have to make do with the life you've been given. In thick and thin. During weal or woe.

— You know, I haven't seen Herr Kaaden since before Degner escaped. Be sure to pass my regards on to him and Mrs. Kaaden. What's her first name, by the way?

— Inge? To be honest, I'm not sure. All I've ever heard is Frau Kaaden.

— Say hello for me, will you?

— As soon as I meet him and the team in London, we'll board the charter for Daytona. There'll be the entire trans-Atlantic flight to make small talk.

— Men talking? What a laugh! You'll be eating or sleeping, most likely. Talk isn't simply grunting a quick hello. It's people connecting, asking about each other's lives. Listening and showing they care. There's nothing small about it. Who else will be on the flight?

— All the big names. Hailwood, Surtees, Anderson, Read, and Mike Duff.

— Not Mrs. Swain? She was written up in yesterday's paper.

— After her showing at the Isle of Man? Not a chance. For the organizers, she was a novelty. A beauty on a bike.

— And a gorgeous one at that.

— She won't be there. *FIM* has stripped her International Racing licence. Says motorcycle racing is too dangerous for women.

— A pity. Beryl Swain's the bravest woman I know. Racing the Isle of Man is not for slouches.

Alan nodded.

— A woman competing in it is unthinkable. The organizers have a point. We're used to men dying in motorsport, but not women. They're the mothers of our children, the objects of our affection. The ones who nurse us back to health when we come home injured and broken.

— Women can be just as addicted to speed as any man and just as reckless.

— Bad luck her 50cc lost its top gear. She limped around Snaefell at 48 mph when she could have been going 80. Then she'd have been with us on the flight to Daytona.

— Could you imagine the headlines?

WOMAN RACES FIRST AMERICAN GRAND PRIX

— No question she's qualified, Alan said.

— It's her choice. She should be allowed to continue. If she qualifies, let her show the world.

— I know what you mean. It's just....I'm all for equality....you know....Women's liberation and all that. But....

— How'd you react if someone told you couldn't follow your dream?

—I'd be angry, I suppose. It's a man's right to choose his own way.

— And a woman's too. It's all about choice and financial independence. Why should a board room of old men decide on the apex of Mrs. Swain's curve? She has the skill to enter a sharp turn at speed and exit safely. She knows better than anyone the line she should follow.

— The Americans want the best riders in the world to compete. That's why they chartered a plane. To get everyone who's anybody on the starting line. There's no prize money to speak of, though. Just a flight, all expenses paid, and the privilege of racing at Daytona.

— Here's hoping some money ends up in your pocket. I'm not sure how much longer we can keep this up. We're going broke with you racing as a privateer.

— I need the points. That's why I'm going. Maybe *Honda* will like my performance. It's my last chance.

— *Honda*'s a good company. They look after their riders.

— They design bikes for the consumer. Built in Japan, for ordinary people to ride. The company is turning the world upside down with its over-engineering. The Europeans and Americans better get ready. In this world, you adapt or go out of business.

— The costs for the Daytona race organizers must be enormous.

— Bill France, Sr. has deep pockets. He wants to make sure that motorcycle racing at the Daytona Speedway becomes a thing. I have to pinch myself. It's unthinkable. In a few days' time, I'll be racing a bike built in East Germany on American soil.

— And a yappy one at that! That Dita has a mind of her own. Does she ever shut up?

— Not for as long as I've known her. She's never left an unspoken thought in her brain.

— There might not be anyone in the stands to hear her mouth off. Is that why Americans prefer car racing to motorcycles? They're quieter?

— Don't think so. They love their V-8s, *Harleys* and *Indians*, too. They can't imagine how small motorcycles engines can be or how fast they can go. Decibels have very little to do with performance. At full throttle, two strokes shriek.

— Like a bike of hornets?

— More like a *caoine* (pronounced caw-wan) of banshees. A keening that warns of imminent death.

— There must be some expats over there. It'd be a good Sunday outing for them. Maybe a few of your fans will fly over. Wouldn't it be loverly if there were eyewitnesses to share your moment in the sun?

— Blooming loverly. A guy could only hope. But my followers aren't doctors and lawyers and such, just workers. Motorcycling has always been the cheaper cousin of auto racing. Not nearly as expensive, but just as thrilling. Death-defying, too. You don't need to spend a lot of money to develop a sudden awareness of your own mortality. The cheapest misstep will do.

— What I hate? How racers risk their lives for one more point in the standings. They don't give a thought about the consequences upon themselves or their loved ones.

— Accidents occur. Riding to the edge clarifies what's important.

— Look what happened to Deg at Suzuka last November. A ball of fire engulfed him. Perris was there when the race officials pulled him away from the flames. How long was he in that Japanese hospital before they shipped him back to Germany? No one thought he'd ever get out. I can't believe he's fit enough to race at Daytona.

— Nothing has ever kept Ernst Degner from competing. He's the best in the world.

— Third-degree burns all over his face. He's horribly disfigured. No matter how abysmally he treated Walter, he doesn't deserve this. I can't imagine he'll ever look himself in the mirror again.

— No question. Women used to clamour after him for his photograph. That won't be happening anymore. However, his contribution to motorsport cannot be denied. But I don't get how he lives with himself.

— At Daytona, he'll be racing at full throttle and so loaded on painkillers, he won't feel a thing.

— At least he's riding a Japanese bike. What with Mr. Kennedy shot, it's hard to imagine the Americans allowing Dita and me to compete. The CIA thinks it was a Communist plot.

— Guess we won't know until Dita clears customs.

They both heard the familiar thrum of a two-stroke *BSA Bantam* pulling up to the front of their house and then a knocking at their door.

Anne rose from the table to answer it.

— Telegram for Mr. Shepherd.

Anne rummaged around her purse for change and gave him a few extra coins. He tipped his hat to her and left. She handed over the telegram.

He read it.

SORRY ALAN CANNOT MAKE DAYTONA WALTER.

— What's going on? Anne asked.

— I don't know.

— You better talk to him.

Alan picked up the phone and asked the operator to place an international call to Walter Kaaden at the motorcycle factory in Zschopau in East Germany. At least in England it wasn't illegal to make calls to Communist countries. Just unusual. The operator put him through without a hitch.

— Hello, Walter. Alan here. Received your telegram What in God's name happened?

— Berlin's refused to grant us travel visas. Tensions after Cuba are too high. Hartmann and the authorities fear that the Americans won't let us in. They don't want to risk any more international embarrassment.

— Bloody politicians. I wish they'd keep their noses out of sport. Athletes want to compete. The Cold War be damned. I can't afford not to race. That's my ticket. I need a factory contract. It's impossible to keep doing this on my own.

Walter interrupted him.

— What are you thinking? I can't see any way out of this.

— I drive to Southend. Load my *Austin J4* onto a cargo plane to Ostend. Then meet you in Marienborn at 0900 tomorrow. Can you get Dita there by then? We'll load her up and drive back across the border—without getting shot—and make it to the airport at Ostend. It's what, 400 miles?

— *Ja*, approximately 600-700 kilometres. I forget exactly.

— That'll give me lots of time after the short flight to drive 35 miles to the London Airport, where the charter is waiting. If I don't have a breakdown.

— I'll do my part. You do yours. *Bis morgen* (See you tomorrow).

They both hung up.

— Looks like I'm going to enter East Germany illegally.

— Don't those trigger-happy soldiers shoot to kill?

— Not always, I hope. I'd like to live another day.

Alan grabbed a handful of pound notes from the jar on the counter and stuffed them into his pocket.

— I'll need these.

She smiled grimly and gave him a hug and a quick kiss for luck.

— Safe trip, she said. Now go! I have a rose garden that needs tending.

She waved him off.

He hurried to the vehicle.

She grabbed her gloves.

Alan jumped into the worn-out driver's seat and the engine rattled to life. It was housed in a thin-walled compartment between the driver and passenger seats, not that Alan noticed the racket. He was used to the ululating expansion chambers on his bike.

The *J4* had a synchromesh transmission with three forward gears. Alan used the clutch only when he started, slowed to a stop, or needed to reverse. Otherwise, he changed from first to second and third and down again by feel, matching the engine rpm to the speed of the gears. Not that precision shifting mattered in a vehicle with a top end of 65 mph.

She was already a high miler when Alan bought her to haul his bikes and tools and give him a cheap place to sleep as he travelled to every track on the Continental Circus. He called her Jenni when he was trying to sweet talk her and Jennie-Four when she had a roadside breakdown. She had a vindictive streak when he pushed her passed her limit. He would have done well had he paid closer attention to her warning signals.

Alan drove to the *British Petroleum* garage down the road. He filled the tank and several jerry cans with petrol. And bought several quarts of oil, just in case the unthinkable happened.

— I'd hate for your bottom to fall out because you ran out of oil.

— That's very thoughtful of you, she replied.

He slipped Jenni into first gear and drove flat out the 300 miles to Southend Airport. She puffed a blue streak and huffed deprecations on him the whole way.

— Bastard, she said. I'm not your German slut. You can't afford to lose my affection, so slow the Hell down.

— I knew you had it in you, Alan replied as he pulled into the departure area. The clock is ticking, and we've got to get on this plane.

— I warn you, Alan Shepherd. You keep this up and you'll be standing by the road with your thumb out, begging for a ride.

— All right, you win, Alan yowled. I'll do whatever you want. On bended knee, I'm yours to love, serve, and obey. Ya, ya, yaaaaa....

He pulled into the airport and bought a return ticket.

Without a minute to spare, the ground crew hauled the *J4* whinging and wheezing up the ramp into the hold of a *British Airways* cargo plane.

Alan had to pee so bad his bladder was bursting. Luckily, he kept a bottle in the back for emergencies like this.

— Need one with a larger neck, he chuckled. This one's too small.

— Idiot, Jenni seethed. Trust you to find some humour in the smallest of things.

The crew chained her down and tossed a gunny sack under her front end.

— We've had experience with this sort of thing before. In case she leaks. That'll make the cleanup a little easier after you're offloaded and on your way.

Jenni dripped some of the oil from her crankcase onto the plane's deck.

— Just do your business. I'm not a vehicle you can trifle with.

52

Grenzkontrolle
(Border Control)

With the first leg of the journey over, Jenni settled down and had a few moments to reflect while the crew prepared the plane for takeoff.

— If Alan backs off, maybe my gaskets will hold. Maybe we'll get there and back in one piece. It's times like these when you wish your driver wasn't one of the fastest racers in the world.

She knew her duties and bore the weight of her responsibility with a heavy heart. She wasn't sure if she was up for the task ahead of her.

— Don't put your all your weight on my pedal, she said as Alan gave the come-along another ratchet, just to be on the safe side. That's all I ask.

Eve may have willingly spanned when Adam eagerly delved, but I'm begging you to act the gentleman. You need to slow down if you want to arrive quickly. This is one of those situations. But I might as well talk until I'm blue in the face. You men are all the same.

Alan didn't have a clue what she was talking about.

The big engines roared, the plane jerked forward, and it accelerated down the runway. At liftoff, the undercarriage clanked up into the hold. The pilot adjusted the flight path and Jenni's world upended.

— What the...? She screamed. Is this the day the music died? Now you've got me flying. You bastard Alan Shepherd! What have you done? I would never have agreed to this had I known.

Alan tried to mollify her. He poured a quart of oil down her gullet and filled her tank from one of the jerry cans in the back. He polished her hubcaps.

— You're doing just fine. The weather's clear. There's not a cloud in the sky. We'll get there safely.

— I hate you, Alan Shepherd. But I love you. You are so infuriating.

Despite her irritation at him, she luxuriated in the cool, clean oil that lubricated her inner workings. A little viscosity goes a long way to soothing a ravaged soul. She closed her eyes and resigned herself to the sleep of the pure in heart.

After the short flight across the English Channel, the ground crew off-loaded the van. Alan drove her as hard as he dared through Belgium, past Aachen and north toward Marienborn, across the border from Helmstedt, east of Hannover. He hoped to enter East Germany without a visa, pick up Dita, and return to the West without causing an international uproar.

— You know you're asking a lot? Jenni said.

— You're right, Alan replied. I have nothing to lose and everything to gain. My life once again is on the line.

— Just go easy on the throttle. Otherwise, you won't have a thing to worry about. Except for Anne's wrath when you get back home broke, me needing repairs you can't afford, and Daytona going ahead without you.

Alan backed off a bit and moaned to a song on the radio. All that I want from you is just a little more loving. Uh huh, baabbbeeee!

Jenni ignored him. With the ungoverned engine no longer straining, she spoke her mind.

—I honestly don't know what you see in that bitch. When there's good patriotic stock in England, bikes that are made right here in Birmingham. Our best racers are winning with *Norton*s and *BSA*s, *AJS* and *Matchless*. But no, you have to fall for that foreign piece of tail. Just a few years back, they were blitzing us into the Third Reich. No wonder Anne's having second thoughts. She's a patient woman, I'll hand her that but, oh my God, you push her to the limit.

— Expansion chambers, Jenni. That's what makes Dita so appealing. The Brits can't touch her.

— Won't touch her more like, she shuddered. And what's with that name, Dita? Is that her model?

— An actress Walter fell in love with when he was growing up. Dita Parlo.

— All right, Alan, just don't drive me like you stole me. Your sweet talk and cool hands caressing my steering wheel will take you much further than your heavy foot. Change my oil, keep my tank topped up, and I'll get you home whenever you call. You've got my attention but know that you're heading straight into a red zone.

Once Alan arrived at the border, he was desperate. He had no choice but to pray that the soldiers guarding the gate would show him some grace. Otherwise, he'd have to meet Walter in Berlin, which he did not have the time for, not if he wanted to get back to Ostend for the flight to England.

Bitte, he said to the young soldier at the *Grenzkontrolle* (border control). I'm Alan Shepherd. I'm racing an *MZ* in the American *Grand Prix* at Daytona. But I need to pick up my bike. It's just across the border. You can see Herr Kaaden from where we are standing. He pointed east. The soldier looked and shook his head.

Ich verstehe es nicht (I don't understand it). *Haben Sie kein Einreisevisum* (Don't you have an entry visa) *oder eine Ausreisegenehmigung* (or an exit permit)? *Ohne ein Visum* (Without a visa) *dürfen Sie in die DDR nicht einreisen* (you cannot enter East Germany without them).

In broken German, Alan did the best he could to explain his situation. When the soldier refused to listen, Alan pleaded with him to call his superior, a man wearing a suit, standing in the shadows.

The soldier waved him over.

Alan repeated himself but emphasized that Walter Kaaden was waiting just across the border.

— *Ich bin auch mit Werner Musiol befreundet,* Alan tried to say (I'm also friends with Werner Musiol).

— *Ich kenne Walter Kaaden und Werner Musiol* (I know Walter Kaaden and Werner Musiol*). Sie müssen einer der ausländischen Fahrer im Rennkollektiv sein.* (You must be one of the foreign riders in the Racing Collective).

— I am.

He handed the officer a signed photograph.

He smiled and nodded his head.

— *Lass ihn durch* (Let him through).

Alan fingered Jenni's gear shift. The two came together into East Germany. He pulled deeply on his cigarette and drove Jenni into the parking lot where Walter was standing with Dita.

— You made it, Walter said.

— Just barely. It was touch-and-go there for a bit. The older border guard's not very sympathetic. His younger superior was, though. I think he's a fan. His eyes brightened when I mentioned you and Werner Musiol.

— Musiol's a hero. Everyone loves him.

— Well, Dita interrupted. You two better get a move on. This isn't a holiday camp. We have kilometres to go before I race. Or should I say miles?

— You haven't changed a bit since I last saw you, have you?

She dismissed him with a sputter.

Alan opened the back door of his van and pulled out an old, battered plank.

— This'll do nicely. He heaved his tool bag up to the front and into the corner, out of the way.

— Just don't mar my finish. I intend to dazzle those Americans with my good looks and new water-cooled 250cc Twin that screams hot at 11,800 rpm. I'll tear up their track at 150 km/h.

— You better learn some American. That's 93 mph in their lingo. An imperial measure much to their republican chagrin.

— That's not exactly what you'd call a funny joke. Don't go into stand up, if you ever have the misfortune of retiring, Alan. It won't end well.

— I'll have to do something, I suppose. Life's too short to sit around and watch other people win all the races.

He pushed Dita up the makeshift ramp and ratcheted down her front forks.

— You're safe and secure for the long trip.

— Aren't you just as sexy as ever? Tying me up like this. I wonder how that Anne ever lets you out of her sight.

She looked at Walter.

— You know, *Onkel. Ich mache nur Spaß* (I'm just joking).

Walter chuckled.

— *Nicht so weit ich sehen kann* (Not as far as I can see).

— *Tschüss*, he said. (Goodbye).

— *Tschüss*, Dita replied. She blew him a kiss that smelled of oil and low-grade benzine.

That was the last time the two old friends ever saw each other again. Both could see that the end was coming but neither knew the day nor the hour.

Alan stowed the plank away and shut the back door. He shook hands with Walter and settled into the driver's seat.

— You'll be fine without me, Walter said. You can strip her engine down as good as anyone I know and put her back together again. Under your hands, she'll be first-rate. You can win this, Alan. *Wir alle brauchen diesen Sieg* (We all need this victory).

Alan slipped Jenni into first gear. She rattled nervously as he eased out the clutch, inching towards the border.

— Now we've got to cross the Iron Curtain without getting shot, she said.

— Jenni! Dita exclaimed. I haven't seen you since Kristianstad. You're looking as *bee-you-tee-full* as ever.

Jenni snorted as Alan put her in gear. She wasn't going to allow that two-wheeled piece of work to upset her payload this early in the journey. She had to get them back on good English soil as quickly as possible.

Walter looked on. The signal lights flashed red as the van left the parking lot. Blue smoke wisped out of the exhaust pipe and fouled the air.

— I don't have a good feeling about this, Jenni said. Those soldiers and their automatic weapons shoot to kill. How do you expect to get across the border this time? You've entered the country illegally, and now you're trying to cross back? You know they use bullets, right?

— One step at a time, pet, Alan said. Try to relax. I'll talk to the soldier, explain the situation, and hope that he doesn't fire on me.

— Us you mean. I'm not immune to bullets. Don't be a bastard, Alan.

— I'll vouch for you Alan, Dita said. You too, Jenni-*vier*. Besides, my German's better than yours.

— Do you honestly think that they have ears to hear a talking motorcycle?

— They listened to a raving Brit, didn't they? They'll listen to me.

Alan rolled down his window as he rolled toward the barrier.

— *Visum, bitte*, the soldier ordered (Visa, please).

He handed him his passport. *Ich habe kein* (I don't have one), Alan attempted to say. Those guards over there let me enter the country, so I could pick up this bike. I'm riding her in America in couple days.

— Pardon? *Sie haben kein Einreisevisum* (You don't have an Entry visa) *oder keine Ausreisegenehmigung* (or an Exit Permit?) *Wie sind Sie jemals hier reingekommen* (How did you ever get in here)? *Es muss in Berlin abgestempelt werden* (It needs to be stamped in Berlin).

— As I said, Alan pleaded with the young officer. I'm racing this East German-made *MZ* in America, but I first to need to catch a flight at Ostend. It leaves at midnight.

The officer could barely understand a word the idiotic Englishman in front of him was saying. He wondered about the international fallout this incident would cause. He hesitated. The man continued babbling on and wouldn't shut up.

His head was spinning. He didn't know what to do.

— The charter to Florida leaves London in the morning. I need to be on that plane.

— Slow down, Alan, Dita said. He doesn't understand a word you are saying.

To calm his racing heart, Alan took a deep breath and breathed out slowly.

— *Offizier*, Dita said. *Wir müssen 700 Kilometer* (Officer, we need to drive 700 kilometres) *vor Mitternacht fahren* (before midnight). *Dieser Van hat schon bessere Tage gesehen* (This van has seen better days). *Können wir mit Ihrem Vorgesetzten sprechen*? (Could we speak to your superior)?

He looked at her blankly and lowered his weapon.

Dita apologized to the young soldier. *Wir hatten keine Zeit nach Berlin zu reisen* (We didn't have the time to travel to Berlin). *Wir fahren Rennen in Amerika* (We are racing in America). *Wir müssen in das Charterflugzeug steigen* (We need to get on the charter plane), *das auf dem Asphalt in London wartet* (that is waiting on the tarmac in London).

The young guard interrupted her.

— *Sie sollten am Eingang des Transitkorridors ein Visum abholen* (You were supposed to pick up a visa at the entry of the Transit Corridor). *Betreten Sie Ostberlin* (Enter East Berlin). *Erledigen Sie Ihre Geschäfte* (Do your business). *Holen Sie sich das abgestempelte Visum* (Get the visa stamped). *Fahren Sie dann zurück in den Westen* (Then drive back to the West), *so wie Sie gekommen sind* (the way you came).

— *Entschuldigen Sie, bitte* (Excuse me, please). *Lassen Sie mich mit Ihrem Kommandanten sprechen* (Let me speak to your Commanding Officer).

Exasperated, the guard waved his superior over. They spoke rapidly.

Alan interrupted.

— Look, I'm Alan Shepherd.

— You're Herr Shepherd?

His English was better than Alan's German.

Alan handed him an autographed glossy photo.

— See? I'm sitting on a *MZ*. I'm on the *Rennkollektiv*. I've competed all over East Germany and western Europe with *MZ*. Surely you recognize me.

— *Ja*, he replied. I know you.

— I'm racing this 250 on American soil. He pointed back to Dita who smiled brightly. Please don't shoot. I'll win the *World Championship* for East Germany. Just let me go. Don't shoot. I have to leave now. I have to be in Ostend before midnight. I'm sorry.

Alan put Jenni into gear and made his way forward. The soldiers watched him cross No-Man's Land. They did not raise their rifles. They waited for the order to shoot, but the man in the suit let them go.

When Alan finally crossed into the West, he and Dita whooped for joy, and Jenni giggled with nervous relief.

— Why they never pulled their triggers, I'll never know, Alan chortled.

The van laughed so hard she farted blue.

— All I know is that I need to pee, Dita said. You'll need to tighten my gaskets before you get to Daytona. Hate to drip some oil on that unsullied American asphalt. They might accuse me of being British.

53

Die Freundlichkeit von Fremden
(The Kindness of Strangers)

Having driven his van flat out from Grange-over-Sands to Southend and just as hard from Ostend to Marienborn, Alan once again floored the pedal. He didn't let up as he hurried west. He needed to catch the midnight plane back to England. He couldn't miss it. His life with Anne depended upon it.

Some two hundred miles from Ostend, somewhere between Cologne and Aachen, Alan wasn't exactly sure; the van's engine exploded.

— You bloody fool, Jenni said. Now you've done it! I told you not to ride me so hard.

An overworked connecting rod banged a hole through the crankcase. Oil poured onto the road below.

Starving, sleep-deprived and distraught, Alan weakened. He had given his all to this venture, robbed Anne's grocery kitty, and wasn't sure how much more he could take.

His life had never looked so bleak.

— Alan! Dita took over. We just passed an Emergency Phone a few hundred metres back. A local tow truck will be on-call. The *ADAC* (*Allgemeiner Deutscher Automobil-Klub*) is affiliated with the British *Automobile Association*. The number will be right there. You are a member, aren't you?

He nodded.

— Ring them. They'll dispatch the nearest driver. Don't panic. Make the call. The fresh air and exercise will do you a wonder. You'll think better once you've calmed down.

Alan obeyed and ran to the phone. Dita was not one to be ignored when she used the imperative.

— Hello? I'm broken down and need a tow, he spoke rapidly into the receiver. He was too upset to try his German. The words tumbled out of his mouth.

The dispatcher didn't fully understand English but caught the gist. She was used to panicky English drivers.

— *Wo sind Sie?* (Where are you?) She spoke slowly and loudly.

— I saw a sign to Eschweiler.

— Eschweiler? *Ja, ich kenne es.* (Yes, I know it). *Zwanzig Minuten, bitte* (Twenty minutes, please).

157

— I have a plane to catch. Please hurry.

He hung up and jogged back to the van. While he waited, he took a leak and smoked a cigarette. Sure could use a bite to eat, he thought as he looked up to the stars shining in the dark sky overhead.

Jenni kept her mouth shut. She felt guilty for the engine failure. Her heart broke to have failed Alan when he needed her most.

A short time later, the tow truck driver pulled in front of the broken down vehicle and put on his flashing lights. He backed the truck up to her bumper and stepped out. He greeted Alan as he walked around the van to assess the situation. Then he chained her up and raised the hoist. He motioned to Alan to get into the cab. He checked his mirrors and pulled out into the driving lane.

— Look, sir. I need to get to Ostend before midnight. Will you tow me there?

— Ostend? *Nein. Ich darf das Auto nur bis zu der nächsten Autowerkstatt schleppen* (I can only tow the car to the nearest garage), *nicht weiter* (not further).

They turned off at the next exit into the village, but the garage was closed.

Alan groaned.

— At this rate, I'll never catch my flight.

— *Kein Problem* (No problem). *Ich kenne den Betreiber* (I know the owner).

He dropped a few coins into the pay telephone and dialed a number. He spoke for a couple of minutes before hanging up.

— *Er wird bald kommen* (He'll come soon).

Then he radioed dispatch to check-in. They gave him a new set of instructions.

Alan poked his head in the window of the van.

— The owner's on his way. Try not to worry. Everything will turn out.

Jenni brooded in silence.

He stepped back as the driver lowered the hoist, unchained the van, and stowed his equipment away. He wished Alan good luck before pulling back onto the Autobahn to rescue another stranded driver.

Sometime later, it seemed an eternity but wasn't, a big old *Mercedes Benz* showed up. The driver got out and they shook hands.

Alan explained who he was and what he was doing.

— Alan Shepherd? *Wirklich* (Really)? The motorcycle racer?

— Yes, that's me.

The big German looked inside the van.

— Is that a new water-cooled 250 Twin?

Dita preened.

— Nun, Sir (Well sir), she said. *Wie nett von Ihnen zu bemerken* (How kind of you to notice).

The owner smiled at her.

— It is. Ain't she a beaut? We've got to get to London before the plane leaves tomorrow morning.

— I'm Erhard Köstler, by the way. A fan. I've followed your career with *MZ*. Saw you at Sachsenring.

— Herr Köstler, a con rod blew apart and my engine is ruined. Can you repair it?

— Not tonight, Herr Shepherd. I don't have any *Austin* parts on hand.

— Could you give me a tow to Ostend? Alan pleaded with him. He was desperate for the kindness of strangers, trusting that this German would be as hospitable as the others he knew.

— I don't have a truck, but your van's light. With that racer in the back, it's not too heavily loaded with gear. I bet this old girl could do the job. He patted the fender of his Merc.

— Not a problem, *Schatzi, Benzi* replied. I'd do almost anything for you. Just put some diesel in my tank before you head out on the highway.

They smiled at each other.

— Are you sure? I don't have much money.

— Just give me your autograph. And win the *GP* in Daytona for the sake of a United Germany. East and west need to be as one.

— I'll do my best.

Alan took out a glossy and signed it.

— That's all I'd expect of any man, or woman, for that matter. He glanced back at Dita. She smiled at him.

They hooked a long chain between the two vehicles.

— I'm sure this is illegal on the Autobahn.

— If we get stopped, I'll explain everything. You're famous in West Germany. The police will understand.

— I'm trying to believe you. My experience with German policemen is that they don't have much of a sense of humour.

— You'll need to be the brakeman. Don't lose your concentration.

— I've done this many times before.

Jenni growled at Alan's insolence. She couldn't believe the indignity she had to endure because of this race against the clock.

When they arrived at Ostend, Herr Köstler bribed a forklift operator to push the van into the cargo hold. He gathered up his chain, watched the plane take off down the runway, and returned home a happy man, satisfied that he had lent a hand to someone in need.

54

Mitten in der Nacht
(In the Middle of the Night)

The plane taxied to a stop near the Southend terminal. Alan released the brake and a couple crewmen gave the van a push. It rolled down the ramp and into the parking lot. At 0200, everything at the airport was shut down. The only light came from the workers unloading the plane. The sky was overcast; the stars snuffed out like candles.

Alan hadn't slept for 42 hours and still needed to get to the London Airport in less than six hours. He couldn't remember the last time he had a bite to eat or a cup of tea.

Jenni was so worried she couldn't speak.

— What am I going to do now? Alan asked.

Dita jumped in.

— Find a telephone and give that *Castrol* guy a call. You know the one I mean.

— Malcolm Edgar?

— Exactly. He must have several vehicles at his disposal.

Alan had a few coins left in his pocket. He found a phone and made the call. Edgar heard the ringing, leapt out of bed, and nearly tripped on the sheet. He stumbled to the phone in the hallway.

— Hello! Edgar here. Who is this? What happened? Is something wrong?

— Malcolm, this is Alan Shepherd. Sorry to call in the middle of the night. I'm at Southend Airport with the *MZ* that I'm to race at Daytona. My van is dead, and I have no way to get to the London airport. The charter leaves at 0800.

— Oh, hello, Alan. Excuse me. What did you say? You're at Southend?

— Do you have someone who can pick me up? I need to get my bike to the London Airport.

— No can do. All my vehicles are in Monte Carlo for the rally. Can you get yourself to the Liverpool Street train station? I have a lorry loaded with tires for the Daytona race. The driver could meet you there and get you to the plane on time.

— Thanks, Malcolm. I'll be out front waiting.

Alan hung up and stared at the leaden sky. His eyes stung red from exhaustion. All the lights in the airport were now turned out. The

160

workers disappeared while he was on the telephone. He could barely think, let alone formulate a plan of action.

— Exactly where is the station from here? He wondered, clueless.

— Head out to the road and flag a car down, Dita ordered. Maybe they'll help.

Alan staggered in the dark out to the deserted road and waited for someone to drive by. A few cars sped by, but none stopped. He had thought he'd hitch a ride into town and get a cab to collect Dita. But no one else was interested in lending a hand to a stranger in the pitch-black night.

Startled, the drivers would see him in their headlights, jerk into the next lane, and hurry to their destinations.

Eventually a police officer saw him, slowed down, and pulled over.

— What are you doing out here alone in the middle of nowhere?

— I'm trying to catch a cab.

— No one will stop for you here. There are too many crazies on the road. Jump in the back. I'll give you a ride to the police station. While he drove, he quizzed Alan, checking his story. He was accustomed to mad dogs and Englishmen going out in the midday sun. But those who ventured out on starless nights? They warranted close scrutiny. When he was satisfied that Alan wasn't a danger, he radioed ahead and arranged to have a cab meet them at the station.

— Take this bloke back to the airport and help him with his luggage. He has a train to catch.

Alan paid the cabbie up front.

— To Southend first? Then the train?

— Yes, Alan explained his predicament. The cabbie sped off into the ink-black night, and Alan settled down into the seat and nodded off in the warmth of the cab.

When the cabbie slowed down, Alan awoke, startled.

— That your van?

Alan nodded.

— Hmm, the cabbie said when he eyed Dita. Not sure she'll fit in.

— What if I keep the door open and hold onto the brake?

— Could work if you kept your grip. Can you do that? I'd hate to have her roll out while I'm going around a bend.

— He's already around the bend, Dita said. I have no intention of joining him.

The cabbie laughed.

— I'll get the two of you to the station. No problem.

— Whatever you do, Alan, Dita said. Hold on. That'd be the death of me, falling out on this deserted highway, cold wind whistling through my frame. This is no country for an unchained East German. If I'm going to meet my demise, I want it to be in America, or Canada, even better. You would too. It's a land of hope for all who toil, the true north strong and free.

Alan's knuckles turned white from his grip on the brake lever.

— You're not going anywhere, dearie.

— *Tschüss, Schatzi!* Dita called out to Jenni.

— Eff off, cow, Jenni replied. You better win, or there's no use coming home. I'll take him back though. Any day of the week. Even on a Sunday. He's my only hope.

She had deep misgivings about being abandoned in this god-forsaken place. The last sight that she had of them were of the cabbie's taillights disappearing into the darkest night of her life.

— I am completely lost and forsaken. Oh God, why have you abandoned me?

When the cabbie pulled up to the station, he wished Alan and Dita good luck for the rest of their journey.

— The next time you're at Southend, could you look in on my van? Tell the authorities I'll be back in a couple of days.

The cabbie nodded.

— I'll be reading the papers for your big win, he said as he drove off to his next fare.

Alan shouldered his bag, rolled Dita up to the wicket, and bought a ticket.

— I'll get one of the porters to help you load the bike, the young woman said. You'll have to ride in the vestibule where the carriages join. This is a commuter train. There's no place for cargo.

Alan found an empty seat and slouched into it, falling to sleep.

— Don't worry, I'll wake you. We Germans like to be on time. I won't let you miss the train.

An hour later, she nudged him awake with her front wheel.

— *Wach auf Schlafmütze* (Wake up, Sleepyhead)! *Wir müssen einen Zug erwischen* (We have a train to catch).

He groaned and shook his head.

— Thanks, Dita, I needed that.

He rolled her to the boarding platform and caught the attention of a baggage porter. When the train stopped, they loaded Dita into the vestibule.

— Good thing she's so light, the porter said. How fast does she go? 155 mph, you say? More like a missile than a motorcycle.

— Keep your hands off my assets, Dita told the porter as he and Alan heaved her aboard.

— I'll talk to my mates. They'll keep an eye out for you and help you off in London.

Alan thanked him and gave him a few coins for his trouble.

Men in suits and women in heels stepped around Alan and Dita as they rushed into the cars looking for seats and wondering what was going on. They were too polite to ask. That bare-to-the-bones motorcycle, that worn-out man, that jumbled bag. What a curiosity. And they wouldn't be satisfied until days later when they read the morning papers on their way to work.

Brit Wins at Daytona GP on Commie Bike!

— So that's who that was! They all exclaimed.

— I knew I'd seen him somewhere, the porter said. I'll never forget that bike. She's a classic.

The train pulled into the Liverpool station, and one of the porters helped Alan lift Dita down to the platform. He rolled her out to the front and saw the Castrol driver waiting for them, just as Edgar promised.

The driver delivered Alan and Dita to the airport 30 minutes before their plane departed. Once Dita was stowed in the cargo hold, Alan boarded the plane and found his seat. He fell asleep and didn't wake until the plane landed in Florida.

55

Langsam Laufen
(Slow Running)

When Alan stepped off the shuttle in Daytona, he couldn't believe how hot it was.

— Must be 80º. I haven't felt this warm since Italy. What a day that was! Second place on a 350 and fourth on a 250.

— Some like it hot, Dita breezed. Walter tuned me up, and I was in fine fettle. It was nice to have him nearby when things got tough. Here we're all alone. No pit crew, no support, it's us against the Yanks. Hope they don't play any tricks.

— Those Americans sure know how to ride.

Dita was skeptical.

— Let's see if they can organize a motorcycle *Grand Prix*.

— From what I read? Bill France, Senior knows what he's doing. He built his customer base hand cranking cars in winter. Gave the owners his business card to call him when they needed repairs. Then he moved to Daytona to escape the Depression. He founded *NASCAR* in 1948. Racing hasn't been the same since.

— You can read? Alan asked her, dumbfounded.

— *Ja! Kann nicht jeder?* (Yes! Can't everyone)?

— So that's where you get your vocabulary. And I thought you were a *Mystical Savant.* Sometimes I can barely understand what you're saying. You use such fancy words.

— What can I say? Dita asked. It's the German in me. The longer the better.

While all the motorcycles and gear were transported to the track, Alan and the other riders checked into their rooms. They had a quick bite to eat and walked to the track to prepare for the first practice run.

— Walter's adjusted the settings for sea level, right?

— Don't be silly. Of course, he has. I made sure. He's only made that mistake once.

Alan smiled. He was about to put Dita to the test.

She cautioned him.

— *Beruhige dich, Junge* (Calm down, lad). We'll pull this off but be patient. Don't let them know how fast I really am. We want to give them the surprise of their lives.

The race official opened the fuel tank to make sure it was empty before filling Dita to the brim. He put some security tape over the cap to make sure it couldn't be opened.

— We don't want any East German shenanigans going on here.

— Me too! I want a level-playing field, Alan said. I'm an athlete, not a cheater. This two-stroke just needs fuel and oil to win.

— *Benzin und Öl* repeated Dita. A good rider and a man like Walter Kaaden at your back. He is the secret to our success. I wish he were here.

— Pardon, said the race official, glancing up from the German motorcycle to the British racer. He thought he heard a woman's voice.

— Just talking to myself. Alan looked sternly at Dita who shut her mouth.

He gave her a bump start and went for a slow practice lap to familiarize himself with the course.

— You're sure not running well, old girl. Was it something you drank? Didn't you get enough sleep on the trip over? You don't have enough power to pull out of fourth gear.

— Stop talking and pay attention. There's something wrong. Walter would be listening. Maybe you should change the magnetos and check the timing.

— I don't understand. He's prepped my bikes before, and they've always run perfectly.

Alan pulled into the pits and stopped near his tools. There were a few fans watching the goings on.

He tore the carburetor apart.

— No dirt, he said. The float is fine.

He put it back together.

— What about the compression?

He rummaged through his bag and found his tester. He took out the spark plug and tightened in the gauge. He turned the engine over and checked the reading.

— Everything's perfect, just the way Kaaden set it up. You're good to go, Dita. You should be running perfectly. Are you ready for the second practice lap?

— Ready as ever.

He started her up and worked his way up through the gears into fourth, but he couldn't get into fifth. The engine ran well in the lower gears but lacked power in the higher ones. What's going on? He wondered as they limped back to the pits in last place.

— At this rate, we won't qualify, Dita said. You need to talk to Walter, or everything we've gone through to get here will be for nothing.

— You're right. I'll give him a call.

He left her in the shade, out of the bright sun, even though she was impervious to the heat, and ran off to the hotel.

He hurried to the counter, sweat pouring off his pale reddened face.

— I'm Alan Shepherd. I'm with the *GP*. I need to call East Germany. Would you put one through for me? There's something wrong with my bike.

The receptionist looked at him, shaking her head.

— I cannot do that, sir. It's illegal for an American to call someone in an eastern bloc country.

— But I'm British, riding an East German motorcycle. I'm here by myself. I don't have any support. Walter Kaaden knows more about this bike than anyone on the planet. He can tell me what's wrong.

But the young woman was adamant. She refused to help this mad Englishman just in from the midday sun, no matter how much he pleaded with her.

— I'm a patriotic American. I am not helping any Communist, and that's final. She stood at attention from behind the counter, turned, and left Alan there alone.

In desperation, Alan searched the hotel for Bill France, Sr. Then he ran back to the track and asked a security guard who pointed towards the office area.

— In there, he said. Big Bill hasn't left his desk in weeks.

— Mr. France, Alan said when he knocked on the door.

— Yes, young man. Call me Big Bill. What can I do for you?

He stepped out from behind his desk. Walk with me. I bet your soul is crying for some cool, clear water. Mine sure is.

Alan blurted out the litany of his engine troubles.

They stopped at the water cooler.

— This'll do us both some good. With their glasses filled, they started back down the hallway to his office.

Alan took a long drink and blathered on.

— Slow down. I can hardly understand you. I may need to get an interpreter in here.

Alan took a breath and started over.

— Sorry sir. I'm here by myself. I don't know what's wrong. My bike's not running properly. I need to talk to the man who set it up for me. He wasn't allowed a visa to leave the country. Otherwise, he'd be here, and we'd solve this problem together.

— I'm sure you would. So, you want to place a phone call to East Germany to figure out what's wrong? Seems reasonable to me. However, as the young lady said, because of all the tension with Russia, it's against the law. Strings have to be pulled.

— Please, sir. If you don't do something for me, I can't compete. I'm desperate.

— All right. Let me make a phone call. I'll see what I can do. I know Mr. Lane in the State Department. He might be able to cut you some slack since you're a foreigner. Maybe he can give you some leeway. Bend the rules as a conciliatory gesture. Show some international cooperation. After all, we're here to race motorcycles, not launch nuclear warheads.

Alan emptied his water glass.

— Wait here.

Bill France, Senior went into his office and searched through his Rolodex. Five minutes later, he beckoned Alan in.

— You can make a three-minute call from here. It'll cost you $20, though.

Alan paid him out of his dwindling supply and spoke to the operator who put the call through to Zschopau.

— Hello Walter, Alan here. I'm having trouble with Dita. She doesn't have enough power to get out of fourth gear.

Walter listened and then interrupted him.

— Stop talking Alan. It sounds as if you've been given the wrong fuel. Is there any way you can change it?

— No. It's the same everybody's getting.

— That's the problem right there. You need to calibrate the timing, points gap, and cylinder compression to the higher octane fuel you've been given. Do you have a piece of paper?

Alan grabbed a pen and a blank sheet of paper from France's desk. He started scribbling. The octane's too high. You'll need to compensate by changing the timing. Remember how to do this? Check the points gap and the disc valves. Also, put an extra base gasket under the cylinders. Do this and....

The line went dead, then a click. Then a dial tone. Then nothing.

Alan looked at the phone. He hung up.

— I can't believe this.

— Did you get what you need?

— Yes, sir. I'll get it sorted. Thanks for everything, Mr. France. Big Bill, I mean.

— Good luck with getting your bike back on the track. I want an American to beat you. No dirty tricks.

— I want to win fair and square.

They shook hands.

Alan hurried back to Dita.

— I know what to do. Walter said it's the fuel.

— I knew those Americans would try to sabotage our run.

— No chicanery here, Dita. It's the same for everyone. East Germany produces a lower octane fuel. It's not about politics. Just firepower. We need to adjust our settings. Tune the carbs and change the cylinder head gasket to match the fuel.

— I hope you're right, Alan. Her heart was in her mouth. I don't want to be cheated out of this race.

Once again, Alan tore Dita's engine apart and adjusted the carburetor settings. Walter had thought of everything. His supply of extra parts included a set of gaskets, O-rings, and sparkplugs. Alan had everything he needed.

— Good thing I trained as a mechanic before I took up carpet laying.

He worked quickly but carefully and made the changes Walter had dictated. He was wiping off his tools when he heard the signal for the last practice lap.

— It's now or never, Dita. Are you going to work this time?

— Only if you followed Walter's instructions perfectly.

— I have. Don't you worry about that.

— Then we better show these Americans what they least expect.

The starter pistol went.

Alan gave Dita a push and popped the clutch. Her engine sprang to life. They rode close to the rear of the other teams to get a feel for the track at near racing speed.

— Don't let them think we're a threat, Dita reminded Alan.

He was too busy manually advancing the spark to reply.

— Just make sure we qualify, Dita whispered.

He blipped the throttle and shot ahead of a few more stragglers making up the rear. He pushed forward and nudged in behind the leaders.

— Slow down.

They loped down the track fast enough to qualify but not raise any alarms.

None of their competitors were the wiser, certain that Alan and his *MZ* were no competition.

— You know, Alan. That felt good. Dawdling. Pretending to be a non-starter.

— Do you think we have them fooled?

— We gave them quite a performance. Might even win an Oscar.

56

Die Letzte Runde
(The Last Lap)

— Hello, a young man shouted from over the fence. You're Alan Shepherd, aren't you?

— Yes, I am.

— Thought so. I notice you're all alone and having a bit of trouble. Want some help?

— Maybe, Alan said. Who are you?

— My name's Vern Simons. I'm a signalman.

— Oh, I see. You know the flags?

— I could be your eyes on the sidelines. Let you know the other riders' positions.

— Pleased to meet you, Vern. Tell the guard at the gate over there that you're with me.

Vern hurried over.

— I'd like to introduce you to Dita. She is the one in charge! If you win her heart, you're in.

— Dita, this is Vern. He says he wants to help.

— Hello, Dita. It's a pleasure to meet you. I saw you at Brands Hatch.

— *Hallo, Herr?*

— Simons.

— *Aus* Steveville? in southern Alberta?

— Yes. How'd you?

— *Ich kenne deine Brüder* (I know your brothers).

— So you're the German *Mädchen* they went on about. You saved their lives. They didn't tell me you were a motorcycle.

— Maybe they were too shellshocked to notice. Certainly taught me enough English to get by. Their plane crash landed, and they parachuted down. They were trying to get to Switzerland.

— They haven't forgotten you, Dita.

— Or me them.

When the race started, Alan stayed near the back. With Vern's help, he spent the first half dozen laps learning the circuit. In the second half, he moved forward, passing one tail pipe of exhaust after another.

It was a high wire act. Alan didn't want to show his hand too quickly, but he didn't want to lag too far behind. However, he was soon familiar enough with the track to catch up to the leaders.

169

He gradually increased his speed and forced those in front to accelerate and protect their positions. When their engines overheated, Dita's ran beautifully, water-cooled, and self-possessed. Once again Walter's innovations brought her to the fore. She was in her element.

One by one, Alan and Dita passed the racers in front until they were the ones leading the pack, not lagging behind.

When the checkered flag came down, they were rocketing across the line, cool running at 152.21 km/h, setting the fastest lap in the race, 1 minute 58 seconds, 94.58 mph.

A British racer on an East German motorcycle winning the 250cc race in the first *Grand Prix* on US soil was not a welcome headline for patriotic Americans. It was a David and Goliath story that no one wanted to read. Cold War tensions muffled the applause that Dita and Alan deserved for their accomplishments against all odds. The East German national anthem was not sung, and its flag was not raised when the medals were given out.

Alan and Dita were given the silent treatment.

But points were points and Alan couldn't be happier. His days living hand-to-mouth as a privateer were numbered. He would soon be racing with *Honda* and have Japanese money to pay into Anne's grocery kitty.

Alan Shepherd was a happy man.

57

Die Offene Straße
(The Open Road)

Alan and Vern rode two-up on Dita to the airport. Alan had slung his ditty bag over his shoulder. It was such a short distance. He figured Vern could ride pillion.

— Just watch those revs, Alan, Dita said. Hey Vern! Don't you want to peel me a ...

— An orange? Alan blanched. No, no, noooooo.

He hammered on the brakes.

Dita laid a strip of rubber in front of the Departure area.

Vern slid forward.

Alan's eyes opened wide.

— I'm screwed, he squeed.

Vern popped off, gushing happily.

— Well, that was quick, he said, his feet firmly planted back on the ground.

— I've got to find me an orchard Alan said. He turned the fuel off.

— They're way back in the other direction, said Vern. You need some for souvenirs, right? Maybe try the Duty Free?

Alan nodded, getting this far and nearly forgetting oranges for Anne was too close for comfort. He had enough of the red zone in his marriage. His mind was onto other things.

The last thing he wanted was to miss the flight back home. He had left a good van in a cold parking lot. Now she was waiting there for him. He needed to haywire her together so they could drive to the Spanish *GP* at Montjuïc in Barcelona.

While he wasn't looking forward to the wrench time a connecting rod engine overhaul in a parking lot demanded, he relished the radiant and hopeful discipline of *Camshaft Sutra* to make him feel one with the universe. Fixing a bike was easier than dealing with the warp of a tightly wound marriage.

It takes all your concentration. Working with tools and fitting parts together, getting them to cooperate. The itty bitty pieces working as one, like a well-oiled machine, leading to a soulful life. The pursuit of happiness in the here and now.

It helps a person forget how hard life can be.

Maybe he should have concentrated more on his marriage. From the get-go, the mistakes newlyweds make ripple outwards. Longlyweds

171

suffer the consequences of youthful indiscretions. They pay the price, cross one bridge, then another, and another, and learn to forgive. If not forget.

But then there's the good. The bountiful harvest of that return is pressed down, shaken together , and overflowing.

Life is what it is.

Dita was eager for the moment of their departure. The rest of her life lay before her. Too wild and precious, it was an open road. Mile after kilometre, she was ready to devour whatever life brought her way, imperial or metric. She understood both.

— You should've been wearing your leathers, Alan said. He slipped off the saddle so that Vern could grab the handlebars. It's safer that way. Motorcycling.

— You and I have covered a lot of blissful kilometres together, Dita sighed, her engine, hot, oily, and ticking.

Super happy and glowing, she quit smoking.

— We have come a long way over the years.

They both knew what was really at stake.

Because of the fiasco with Degner, Dita would soon be left out in the cold. Her track days were over. It was time for her to retire.

— Are you certain about this, Dita? There's still a berth in the cargo hold for you.

—Would you like to see me on display in a museum shining and polished? To be ogled at? I'm a female. I want to ride and live and love. Nothing can stop my engine. It needs roaring across this land. I haven't been surer of anything in my whole life. The Iron Curtain is drawn but I'm ready to fly out the window. There's a land of pronghorn antelope, short grass, and sage, a place that has my heart, where I can sing. From horizon to horizon, with nary a mountain, hill, or tree to block my view. It's the open road that I love.

— Don't you worry yourself, Mr. Shepherd, Vern said. I'll keep her out of the red zone. I'll look after her.

— With that haircut? Are you kidding me? You know she's a trickster, right?

— I twist wrenches at the Suffield British Army Block in southern Alberta. I'm used to things being harder than they need to be. She'll be in good hands, I promise you.

— But will you be? Unravelling the myth that they call German engineering?

— It's a rat's nest, I agree. But the Japanese are currently unravelling its mystery, one bewildering snarl at a time. If I can repair *Lucas* wiring and convince a big old *Norton* to start, I can handle whatever japery, flimflammery, and tomfoolery Dita foists on me.

— You two better quit your chirping, Dita said, blushing. Alan, you have a plane to catch. Vern?

— We have concert tickets to buy. The Beatles have landed. We've got to get to the Coliseum in Washington. They're playing on the eleventh.

— That's in a week, Dita said. Is there snow in the forecast?

— Shouldn't be a problem, Alan said. Him being from Canada and all.

— You do know how to ride in the snow, don't you Laverne Simons?

— Only my mother calls me that, and only when she's annoyed.

Dita already knew exactly where and how to get his goat.

— I'm a fair-weather motorcyclist. That's why I'm here in Florida, looking for a fine woman to keep me warm. Those long winter nights don't get any easier. Besides, your racing slicks aren't good for anything other than dry pavement.

— Hey! I've won races in downpours. I suppose I could try a new set of treads, maybe hand-inspected *Dunlops*, Made In America. A gal can always use one more pair.

Tires, maybe. Vern understood that, but shoes? Vern hadn't once given his a second thought. He just wore the life out of them.

When he wasn't racing, Alan wore work boots. Most comfortable things he owned. It didn't help when he was on the dance floor with Anne, though. She winced every time. She preferred to lead and follow with her girlfriends. It's safer that way. Dancing.

— Maybe we should head for the nearest train station, Vern suggested. Ride in style. What do you say? Go first-class?

Dita looked at Alan.

— What have I gotten myself into?

— I was wondering that very thing myself.

— There's no turning back, eh Dita. Let's witness the invasion firsthand. Guitars and drum kits instead of muskets and field cannon, not to mention mop tops. He shook his head. The British are a-coming. They want to recapture their old colony, as musicians this time, not Lobster-Backs.

Vern settled into Dita's saddle. He opened the petcock and made sure that the *Kill* switch was in the Off position and the *Ignition* was in the On. Alan gave Dita an affectionate push, Vern popped the clutch, and Dita's engine came to life, proclaiming its intent to eat up as much of the road as possible.

Alan bought a bag of oranges from a kiosk as the two headed for the station. He made sure the bag said *Grown in Florida* before running to catch his plane.

Vern and Dita had to catch the *East Coast Champion, Diesel Number 1019.* Ride it First Class all the way.
— Dita screeched *Er liebt mich, ja, ja-ja, jajaja, jaaaaaaaaa.*

THE END

Acknowledgements

I wrote *Dita* after surviving the worst that the cancer ward had to offer.

Thank you to everyone at the Cross Cancer Institute in Edmonton, Alberta for giving me your best.

I am grateful to Dr. Andrew Belch, Dr. Ross Lindskoog, and Dr. Irwindeep Sandhu for their care. I am alive because of them.

Multiple Myeloma rages on like a lion, but research keeps it at bay.

Thank you to Caterina Edwards, Glen Huser, John Keeble, and Keith Liggett for reading my early work and encouraging me. You introduced me to the writer's life.

Thank you to Joachim Bürgschwentner and Ilona Ryder for your friendship and for triple checking the German in this text. All the mistakes that remain are mine.

Thank you to Ronnene Andersen, Cheryl and Gary Krueger, Tom Pedersen, and Maria Scala for wrestling my rough drafts to the ground. If my work is readable, it is because of your input. Thank you to Mark Whitehouse and *Moto-Kul:ture* Magazine for publishing the early chapters.

I have a cadre of retired, old men who like to nitpick that bear mentioning. Their wives say it's because they have nothing better to do. Sib, Suzan, and Carolyn, I did what I could to divert their attention for a few short hours. Thank you Fred Clark, Eldon Evans, and Andrew Gutteridge for going through my work with a fine tooth comb. You were there when I needed extra eyes. Any mistakes that remain are entirely Dita's fault. It's her penchant, messing with our heads and frustrating the ways of riders, writers, and readers. This one in particular.

Thank you to my close friends upon whom I foisted drafts over the years. Your names are legion. I cannot name you all because I'd forget one and that would be terrible. You are loved.

The way musicians need audiences to complete a performance, so writers need readers to respond to their work. It is part of the creative process. You were there for me, and I will never forget you.

Bibliography

Michelle Ann Duff, *The Mike Duff Story: Make Haste, Slowly*. mad8 publishing, 1999.

Mat Okley, *Stealing Speed: The Biggest Spy Scandal in Motorsport History*. Haynes Publishing, 2009.

Mick Phillips, "Alan Shepherd," *Classic Bike*, July 1999.

"The YA-1 Story (Part 2): The Seven Samurai, 180 Hard Days in the Prototyping Workshop." global.yamaha-motor.com

Mick Walker, *German Motorcycles*. Osprey Publishing, 1989.

---. *German Racing Motorcycles*. Redline Books, 1999.

Wikipedia.

Manfred Woll, *IFA / MZ Renngeschichte* 1949-1961. HEEL Verlag, 2001.

The facts may be in the public domain, but the fantasy is mine.
I have so intertwined the two that they are almost inseparable.
This is a story true enough for the telling.
It is a work of the imagination for your enjoyment.

No motorcycles were damaged in its writing.

www.ingramcontent.com/pod-product-compliance
Lightning Source LLC
Chambersburg PA
CBHW061214210726
48294CB00006B/1836